OTHELLO,
THE MOOR OF
VENICE

William Shakespeare

INTRODUCTION BY
NED HALLEY

Collector's Library

This edition published in 2011 by
Collector's Library
an imprint of CRW Publishing Limited,
69 Gloucester Crescent, London NW1 7EG

ISBN 978 1 907360 13 8

Text and Introduction copyright ©
CRW Publishing Limited 2011

2 4 6 8 10 9 7 5 3

Typeset in Great Britain by
Bookcraft Ltd, Stroud, Gloucestershire

Printed and bound in China by Imago

Collector's Library

OTHELLO,
THE MOOR OF VENICE

Contents

Introduction

Beware the green-eyed monster. The phrase seems so much of the present, a breezy caution against a rampant vice. But what is now such an everyday idiom had its first outing in another age altogether. It has glowed emerald bright for more than four centuries from the pages of *Othello*, Act III Scene 3:

> O, beware, my lord, of jealousy;
> It is the green-eyed monster which doth mock
> The meat it feeds on

The speaker is Iago, most malevolent of all Shakespeare's villains, co-opting the allegory of the cat that torments its prey to warn Othello against the very sin he is inducing his unwitting master to commit: the delusion that his wife is betraying his love. Jealousy – insane, murderous jealousy – is at the heart of this remorseless tragedy.

William Shakespeare wrote it mid-career in 1602–03, after *Hamlet* and before *King Lear* in the series of immortal tragedies he created in his late thirties and early forties. Like so many of the plays, Othello has an Italian setting, and is based on an Italian story. The source was *Un Capitano Moro*, a novella of 1565 by Giovanni Battista Giraldi, a poet and novelist who wrote under the pen-name Cinthio. The story, included in Cinthio's *Hecatommithi* (100 myths), a collection of tales along similar lines to Boccaccio's better-known *Decameron* of two centuries earlier. Some scholars have claimed that the *Capitano* was based on a series of actual crimes that took place in Venice in 1508. Whatever the case, Shakespeare's version echoes the story quite closely, although Cinthio's Moorish Captain is much more a villain of the piece. He does not murder Desdemona himself, but delegates the task to his ensign (Iago, who in Cinthio's version is infatuated with, and rejected by, Desdemona) with whom he then conspires to cover up the crime by the unlikely means of collapsing a ceiling on to the body to make it appear she died accidentally. It not until after committing this foul deed that Othello and Iago embark on their mutual destruction. Desdemona (from Greek, meaning wretched, and thus doomed) is the only name lifted by Shakespeare from Cinthio. All other names in the cast of *Othello*, along with the key characters Brabantio and Roderigo, as well as some minor parts, appear to be of Shakespeare's invention.

The poetry and narrative drive of *Othello* are the recognisable signatures of the Bard. The story breathes rancour and revenge from the outset as Iago in the opening exchange of the play, night-time in a Venice street, pours out to Roderigo his resentment at being passed over for promotion by Othello, a commander in the army of the Republic. For his new lieutenant, the Moor's choice is 'one Michael Cassio, a Florentine … that never set a squadron in the field' while he, Iago, had fought alongside Othello against the Turks at Rhodes and Cyprus and yet is left in the role of 'his Moorship's ancient.' Here, ancient means not an old man – Iago later tells us he is only twenty-eight – but an ensign, the lowest commissioned military rank.

Iago's self-regard ('I know my price, I am worth no worse a place') and bitterness already betray his own flawed character. Roderigo might be taken in by the bile – he would rather be the Moor's hangman than his ensign, he avers – but we now begin to suspect why Othello might have passed over this surly underling. Suspicion turns to certainty as Iago moves seamlessly into revenge mode. He will deceive his master without scruple:

> … I will wear my heart upon my sleeve
> For daws to peck at: I am not what I am.

Iago knows Othello has secretly married Desdemona, and urges Roderigo, her unrequited suitor, to injure the Moor by revealing the news to her father Brabantio, a powerful senator. 'Rouse him: make after him, poison his delight,' Iago says, and Roderigo eagerly obliges, shouting up at the senator's window. When Brabantio appears, and demands to know who Iago is, the profane wretch (as Brabantio has already called him for earlier insinuations) blithely tells him:

> I am one, sir, that comes to tell you your daughter
> and the Moor are now making the beast with two backs.

It's one of the nastiest rejoinders in all of Shakespeare, and fit to make audiences gasp. Thus, all in Act I Scene 1, do we make the acquaintance of the villain and his intentions, and begin the roller-coaster ride that this fearsome play turns out to be.

The setting for the play was topical in its own time. The main action takes part in Cyprus rather than Venice, as Othello is sent to the island to lead the forces of the Republic against an imminent invasion by the 'Ottomites'. This is, in fact, a partial replay of the actual events that had taken place thirty years earlier in 1570. Cyprus became part of the Venetian Empire in 1489, and was constantly raided by the Ottoman Turks, who considered this offshore outpost a threat to their trade and security.

The Turks finally got a foothold in 1570 by capturing the capital city, Nicosia, amid terrible bloodshed. But it was to be 1571 before the island fell wholly under Ottoman control, thanks to the resistance of the Venetian garrison at the port of Famagusta. Under the command of Captain-General Marco Antonio Bragadin, about 6,000 Venetian troops kept at bay an Ottoman force estimated at 100,000, supported by 150 ships, for almost a year. Finally overwhelmed, Bragadin surrendered. His officers were hanged, and Bragadin himself was publicly tortured and flayed alive by his captors in the Famagusta docks. His skin was then stuffed with straw and the macabre figure paraded through the streets of the town before being dispatched to Istanbul for the delectation of the Sultan.

This horrible incident would have been well-known to William Shakespeare, and he may have had Bragadin in mind when creating the courageous character of Othello, destined to face the Ottomans at Cyprus. But in the play no conflict ensues. By the time Othello, accompanied by his wife as well as his officers, reaches the island the Turkish fleet has been dispersed by a storm in a manner reminiscent of the fate of the Spanish Armada, much of which had foundered off the British coast in 1588. Not that the Ottoman navy was infallible. In October 1571, most of the fleet was destroyed by a Christian alliance, led by the Venetians, at Lepanto off the coast of Greece. This last great sea battle between oar-powered galleys effectively ended two centuries of Ottoman naval dominance in the eastern Mediterranean.

In the play, while the Ottoman menace retreats, the lethal intentions of Iago take centre stage. Frustrated in his attempt to put Othello in bad blood with his father-in-law, whose rage at the elopement evaporated on learning from his daughter how her heart had been won, the ensign encourages the ever-biddable Roderigo to pursue Desdemona, assuring him she will tire of the Moor soon enough. And when he has packed Roderigo off to sell his lands in order to fund his hopeless suit, Iago begins to hatch a further plot, concerning his rival Cassio. On the one hand, he will insinuate to Othello that his handsome new lieutenant 'is too familiar with his wife'. And on the other, he will tell Roderigo that Cassio is in love with Desdemona.

All the while, Othello expresses his trust in his ensign. 'Honest Iago,' he declares at every turn. 'Iago is most honest,' he says on retiring with Desdemona to bed on the first night ashore at Cyprus and bidding goodnight to the ensign and Cassio. Iago immediately sets about getting the young lieutenant drunk, knowing he will lose control. He does, and starts a swordfight with Roderigo, all engineered

by Iago, in which Montano, the Cyprus governor, inter-
venes and is wounded by Cassio. Othello, roused by the
hubbub, is outraged and strips Cassio of his rank. But Iago
is not satisfied. Taking the desolate Cassio aside, he
persuades him to ask Desdemona to plead with the Moor
for his reinstatement.

It is an unrelenting vortex of evil, animated by Iago's
searing soliloquies of satisfaction with his progress, contemplation of his next wickedness, and self-congratulation on
what he perceives to be the justice of his cause. Having
convinced Cassio to make a fatal approach to Desdemona
the next morning, he is wished by his victim 'Good night,
honest Iago' and turns to the audience:

> And what's he then that says I play the villain?
> When this advice is free I give and honest

It is just one of numerous points in the play in which
Iago's devilry veers perilously close to pantomime. To his
reiterated claims that he is honest, any audience could be
forgiven for shouting out 'Oh no you're not!' Perhaps the
playwright hoped they would.

In Act III, Iago continues the inexorable process,
persuading Othello of Desdemona's infidelity by spinning
Cassio's entirely innocent dealings with her into a fantasy
of shameless trysting. Iago even resorts to claiming that
sleeping next to Cassio one night but kept awake by a
toothache, he had happened to hear the lieutenant's night-
time ravings:

> In sleep I heard him say 'Sweet Desdemona,
> Let us be wary, let us hide our loves;'
> And then, sir, would he gripe and wring my hand,
> Cry 'O sweet creature!' and then kiss me hard,
> As if he pluck'd up kisses by the roots
> That grew upon my lips: then laid his leg
> Over my thigh, and sigh'd, and kiss'd; and then
> Cried 'Cursed fate that gave thee to the Moor!'

It is one of the moments of the play in which we might ask, who does Iago think he's kidding? Othello is an intelligent man of the world in love with his wife. He must be fully aware that his ensign might resent the officer who was promoted over his head. He has seen no material evidence of an affair. But he believes this fantastic sleeptalking story: 'O monstrous! monstrous!' he howls.

Is it a flaw in Shakespeare's characterization of the Moor that he renders him so gullible? We can all draw our own conclusions, of course, and scholars have argued unendingly over the matter of whether Othello is paranoid on account of his race, a fantasist or a fool, a masochist or a maniac. Iago, for his own part, does not seem to think Othello is any of these. He even doubts whether he can count on corrupting the marriage:

> The Moor, howbeit that I endure him not,
> Is of a constant, loving, noble nature,
> And I dare think he'll prove to Desdemona
> A most dear husband.

But the villain does not let this reluctant regard stand in his way. Othello has other weaknesses to exploit. Vanity comes into it. The great Cambridge literary critic F.R. Leavis famously opined that 'A habit of approving self-dramatisation is an essential element in Othello's make-up, and remains so at the very end . . . contemplating the spectacle of himself, Othello is overcome with the pathos of it.'

But Shakespeare does not, finally, rest the case wholly on Iago's wild inventions. In the ploy with the treasured handkerchief, unwittingly dropped by Desdemona, purloined for Iago by his blameless (if naive) wife Emilia and planted in Cassio's quarters, the villain introduces what appears to be substantive proof of a relationship. In Act IV, as the handkerchief is produced by Cassio's lover Bianca with the fatal words 'this is some minx's token,' Desdemona's fate is sealed.

The killing begins in Act V in a remorseless dénouement of the tragedy. It is neat that Roderigo, the first victim of

Iago's wiles, becomes the first to realize he has been duped, and is the first to die, finished off by the villain before he can expose the crime. Now Othello tells Desdemona she will die, and is deaf to her pleas. Cassio, he says, has admitted adultery and will be dead before he can confess any further:

> No, his mouth is stopp'd
> Honest Iago has ta'en order for't

And so Desdemona is killed without knowing the truth. Emilia is next, stabbed by her husband after exposing his ruse with the handkerchief, and confronting Othello with the full horror of his misjudgement. The Moor, in his turn, dies knowing what he has done, but not why. Before he stabs himself, he claims to have been 'an honourable murderer ... for nought I did in hate, but all in honour' and demands to know from Iago what he has done to deserve it all. Iago shows no remorse:

> Demand me nothing: what you know, you know:
> From this time forth I never will speak word.

In the final moments of the play, the guilt of Othello suddenly seems to match even that of the monstrous villain himself. Perhaps it is true. This is not a tragedy that ends on any kind of redemptive note, but the circle is certainly completed. In the modern post-catastrophe cliché, lessons will be learned.

The enduring appeal of the play must owe much to the message that jealousy is a dangerous motivator whose consequences can get rapidly out of control. The theme largely subsumes the difficult racist element in the play, which in modern times might have seriously diminished its popularity.

Since its first recorded performance, on 1 November 1604 in the Banqueting House at Whitehall Palace in London, quite possibly with King James I in the audience, *Othello* has proved a perpetual attraction. It was staged regularly throughout the seventeenth century and in 1660 was seen at the Cockpit theatre by Samuel Pepys. Later in that year, a performance of the play by the King's Company made history by featuring Margaret Hughes in the role of Desdemona. She was the first professional actress ever to appear, at least officially, in an English theatre.

A new landmark was reached in 1833, when Ira Aldridge became the first black actor to appear in the title role on a London stage. America did not catch up until 1943 when Paul Robeson, who had first played Othello in London a decade earlier, with Peggy Ashcroft as Desdemona, finally appeared in a Broadway production with an otherwise all-white cast lead by José Ferrer as Iago. Hitherto in the US, thanks to peculiar race-relations customs, Othello had been performed only by casts comprising actors of one colour or the other. Robeson's production ran to 296 performances, the greatest number for any Shakespeare play ever staged on Broadway.

Robeson, revered by audiences and critics alike for his portrayal of the Moor as well as for his other stage, singing and screen work, never filmed *Othello*. The first memorable movie was made by the cast who first performed the play at the National Theatre in London in 1964, lead by Sir Laurence Olivier with Frank Finlay as Iago and Maggie Smith as Desdemona. The film, released in 1965, was in effect a recording of the National Theatre version, and had a mixed reception from the critics, some of whom decried the casting of a white actor, however distinguished, in the title role. Elsewhere, praise was lavished, and Othello remains the only film to have received four acting nominations (those mentioned plus Joyce Redman as Emilia) for Oscars.

The play has twice been adapted for major operas, first by Gioacchino Rossini in 1816. But Giuseppi Verdi's *Otello* has eclipsed the former since its triumphant première on the stage of La Scala, Milan, on 5 February, 1887. There are numerous critics who count *Otello* as Verdi's masterpiece.

In the present century, the play continues to be prolifically performed. It was filmed in 2007 with Laurence Fishburn as the Moor and Kenneth Branagh as Iago, and in 2009 a series of memorable performances was given by the popular British comedian Lenny Henry in the title role at the West Yorkshire Theatre in Leeds. The critics were enthusiastic. 'This is one of the most astonishing debuts in Shakespeare I have ever seen,' wrote Charles Spencer in *The Daily Telegraph*. 'It is impossible to praise too highly Henry's courage in taking on so demanding and exposed a role, and then performing it with such authority and feeling.'

CASSIO Madam, I'll take my leave.

OTHELLO, THE MOOR OF VENICE

DRAMATIS PERSONAE

DUKE OF VENICE.
BRABANTIO, a *senator*.
OTHER SENATORS.
GRATIANO, *brother to a Brabantio*.
LODOVICO, *kinsman to Brabantio*.
OTHELLO, *a noble Moor in the service of the Venetian state*.
CASSIO, *his lieutenant*.
IAGO, *his ancient*.
RODERIGO, *a Venetian gentleman*.
MONTANO, *Othello's predecessor in the government of Cyprus*.
CLOWN, *servant to Othello*.

DESDEMONA, *daughter to Brabantio and wife to Othello*.
EMILIA, *wife to Iago*.
BIANCA, *mistress to Cassio*.

SAILOR, MESSENGER, HERALD, OFFICERS,
GENTLEMEN, MUSICIANS, *and* ATTENDANTS.
SCENE — *Venice: a seaport in Cyprus*.

BRABANTIO What is the reason of this terrible summons?

ACT I

SCENE I

Venice. A street.

Enter RODERIGO *and* IAGO.

RODERIGO

Tush, never tell me; I take it much unkindly
That thou, Iago, who hast had my purse
As if the strings were thine, shouldst know of this,—

IAGO

'Sblood, but you will not hear me:—
If ever I did dream of such a matter,
Abhor me.

RODERIGO

Thou told'st me thou didst hold him in thy hate.

IAGO

Despise me, if I do not. Three great ones of the city,
In personal suit to make me his lieutenant,
Off-capp'd to him:—and, by the faith of man,
I know my price, I am worth no worse a place:—
But he, as loving his own pride and purposes,
Evades them, with a bombast circumstance
Horribly stuff'd with epithets of war;
And, in conclusion,
Nonsuits my mediators; for, 'Certes,' says he,
'I have already chose my officer.'
And what was he?
Forsooth, a great arithmetician,
One Michael Cassio, a Florentine,
A fellow almost damn'd in a fair wife;
That never set a squadron in the field,
Nor the division of a battle knows
More than a spinster; unless the bookish theoric,
Wherein the toged consuls can propose
As masterly as he: mere prattle, without practice,
Is all his soldiership. But he, sir, had th'election:
And I—of whom his eyes had seen the proof
At Rhodes, at Cyprus, and on other grounds
Christian and heathen—must be be-lee'd and calm'd
By debitor and creditor; this counter-caster,
He, in good time, must his lieutenant be,
And I—God bless the mark!—his Moorship's ancient.

RODERIGO

By heaven, I rather would have been his hangman.

IAGO

Why, there's no remedy; 'tis the curse of service,
Preferment goes by letter and affection,
And not by old gradation, where each second
Stood heir to th'first. Now, sir, be judge yourself,
Whether I in any just term am affined

To love the Moor.

RODERIGO

                I would not follow him, then.

IAGO

O, sir, content you;
I follow him to serve my turn upon him:
We cannot all be masters, nor all masters
Cannot be truly follow'd. You shall mark
Many a duteous and knee-crooking knave,
That, doting on his own obsequious bondage,
Wears out his time, much like his master's ass,
For naught but provender; and, when he's old, cashier'd:
Whip me such honest knaves. Others there are,
Who, trimm'd in forms and visages of duty,
Keep yet their hearts attending on themselves;
And, throwing but shows of service on their lords,
Do well thrive by them, and, when they have lin'd their coats,
Do themselves homage: these fellows have some soul;
And such a one do I profess myself.
For, sir,
It is as sure as you are Roderigo,
Were I the Moor, I would not be Iago:
In following him, I follow but myself;
Heaven is my judge, not I for love and duty,
But seeming so, for my peculiar end:
For when my outward action doth demonstrate
The native act and figure of my heart
In compliment extern, 'tis not long after
But I will wear my heart upon my sleeve
For daws to peck at: I am not what I am.

RODERIGO

What a full fortune does the thick-lips owe,
If he can carry't thus!

IAGO

                Call up her father,

Rouse him:—make after him, poison his delight,
Proclaim him in the streets; incense her kinsmen:
And though he in a fertile climate dwell,
Plague him with flies; though that his joy be joy,
Yet throw such changes of vexation on't,
As it may lose some colour.

RODERIGO

Here is her father's house; I'll call aloud.

IAGO

Do; with like timorous accent and dire yell
As when, by night and negligence, the fire
Is spied in populous cities.

RODERIGO

What, ho, Brabantio! Signior Brabantio, ho!

IAGO

Awake! what, ho, Brabantio! thieves! thieves! thieves!
Look to your house, your daughter, and your bags!
Thieves! thieves!

      BRABANTIO *appears above, at a window.*

BRABANTIO

What is the reason of this terrible summons?
What is the matter there?

RODERIGO

Signior, is all your family within?

IAGO

Are your doors lock'd?

BRABANTIO

            Why, wherefore ask you this?

IAGO

Zounds, sir, y' are robb'd; for shame, put on your gown;
Your heart is burst, you have lost half your soul;
Even now, now, very now, an old black ram
Is tupping your white ewe. Arise, arise;
Awake the snorting citizens with the bell,
Or else the devil will make a grandsire of you:
Arise, I say.

BRABANTIO
           What, have you lost your wits?

RODERIGO
Most reverend signior, do you know my voice?

BRABANTIO
Not I: what are you?

RODERIGO
My name is Roderigo.

BRABANTIO
           The worser welcome:
I have charg'd thee not to haunt about my doors:
In honest plainness thou hast heard me say
My daughter is not for thee; and now, in madness,
Being full of supper and distempering draughts,
Upon malicious bravery, dost thou come
To start my quiet;—

RODERIGO
Sir, sir, sir, —

BRABANTIO
           But thou must needs be sure
My spirit and my place have in them power
To make this bitter to thee.

RODERIGO
                 Patience, good sir.

BRABANTIO
What tell'st thou me of robbing? this is Venice;
My house is not a grange.

RODERIGO
              Most grave Brabantio,
In simple and pure soul I come to you.

IAGO
Zounds, sir, you are one of those that will not serve
God, if the devil bid you. Because we come to do you
service, and you think we are ruffians, you'll have your
daughter cover'd with a Barbary horse; you'll have your
nephews neigh to you; you'll have coursers for cousins,
and gennets for germans.

BRABANTIO

What profane wretch art thou?

IAGO

I am one, sir, that comes to tell you your daughter and
  the Moor are now making the beast with two backs.

BRABANTIO

Thou art a villain.

IAGO

     You are — a senator.

BRABANTIO

This thou shalt answer: I know thee, Roderigo.

RODERIGO

Sir, I will answer any thing. But, I beseech you,
If't be your pleasure and most wise consent,
As partly I find it is, that your fair daughter,
At this odd-even and dull watch o'the night,
Transported, with no worse nor better guard
But with a knave of common hire, a gondolier,
To the gross clasps of a lascivious Moor, —
If this be known to you, and your allowance,
We then have done you bold and saucy wrongs;
But, if you know not this, my manners tell me
We have your wrong rebuke. Do not believe
That, from the sense of all civility,
I thus would play and trifle with your reverence:
Your daughter, — if you have not given her leave, —
I say again, hath made a gross revolt;
Tying her duty, beauty, wit, and fortunes,
In an extravagant and wheeling stranger
Of here and every where. Straight satisfy yourself:
If she be in her chamber or your house,
Let loose on me the justice of the state
For thus deluding you.

BRABANTIO

     Strike on the tinder, ho!
Give me a taper! — call up all my people! —
This accident is not unlike my dream:

Belief of it oppresses me already. —
Light, I say! light! [*Exit above.*

IAGO

                Farewell; for I must leave you:
It seems not meet, nor wholesome to my place,
To be produc'd — as, if I stay, I shall —
Against the Moor: for, I do know, the state,
However this may gall him with some check,
Cannot with safety cast him; for he's embark'd
With such loud reason to the Cyprus wars,
Which even now stand in act, that, for their souls,
Another of his fadom they have none
To lead their business: in which regard,
Though I do hate him as I do hell-pains,
Yet, for necessity of present life,
I must show out a flag and sign of love,
Which is indeed but sign. That you shall surely find him,
Lead to the Sagittary the raised search;
And there will I be with him. So, farewell. [*Exit.*

    Enter, below, BRABANTIO, *with* SERVANTS *and*
                torches.

BRABANTIO

It is too true an evil: gone she is;
And what's to come of my despised time
Is naught but bitterness. — Now, Roderigo,
Where didst thou see her? — O unhappy girl! —
With the Moor, say'st thou? — Who would be a father! —
How didst thou know 'twas she? — O, she deceives me
Past thought! — What said she to you? — Get more
    tapers;
Raise all my kindred. — Are they married, think you?

RODERIGO

Truly, I think they are.

BRABANTIO

O heaven! — How got she out? — O treason of the
    blood! —

Fathers, from hence trust not your daughters' minds
By what you see them act. — Is there not charms
By which the property of youth and maidhood
May be abused? Have you not read, Roderigo,
Of some such thing?

RODERIGO

              Yes, sir, I have indeed.

BRABANTIO

Call up my brother. — O, would you had had her! —
Some one way, some another. — Do you know
Where we may apprehend her and the Moor?

RODERIGO

I think I can discover him, if you please
To get good guard, and go along with me.

BRABANTIO

Pray you, lead on. At every house I'll call;
I may command at most. — Get weapons, ho!
And raise some special officers of night. —
On, good Roderigo; — I'll deserve your pains.   [*Exeunt.*

SCENE II

Another street.

Enter OTHELLO, IAGO, *and* ATTENDANTS
with torches.

IAGO

Though in the trade of war I have slain men,
Yet do I hold it very stuff o'the conscience
To do no contriv'd murder: I lack iniquity
Sometimes to do me service: nine or ten times
I had thought t'have yerk'd him here under the ribs.

OTHELLO

'Tis better as it is.

IAGO

            Nay, but he prated,
And spoke such scurvy and provoking terms

Against your honour,
That, with the little godliness I have,
I did full hard forbear him. But, I pray you, sir,
Are you fast married? Be assured of this,
That the magnifico is much beloved;
And hath, in his effect, a voice potential
As double as the duke's: he will divorce you;
Or put upon you what restraint and grievance
The law — with all his might t'enforce it on —
Will give him cable.

OTHELLO

              Let him do his spite:
My services which I have done the signiory
Shall out-tongue his complaints. 'Tis yet to know, —
Which, when I know that boasting is an honour,
I shall promulgate, — I fetch my life and being
From men of royal siege; and my demerits
May speak, unbonneted, to as proud a fortune
As this that I have reach'd: for know, Iago,
But that I love the gentle Desdemona,
I would not my unhoused free condition
Put into circumscription and confine
For the sea's worth. But, look! what lights come yond?

IAGO

Those are the raised father and his friends:
You were best go in.

OTHELLO

              Not I; I must be found:
My parts, my title, and my perfect soul
Shall manifest me rightly. Is it they?

IAGO

By Janus, I think no.

    Enter CASSIO, *and certain* OFFICERS *with torches.*

OTHELLO

The servants of the duke, and my lieutenant. —
The goodness of the night upon you, friends!
What is the news?

CASSIO
                The duke does greet you, general;
And he requires your haste-post-haste appearance
Even on the instant.

OTHELLO
                What is the matter, think you?

CASSIO
Something from Cyprus, as I may divine:
It is a business of some heat: the galleys
Have sent a dozen sequent messengers
This very night at one another's heels;
And many of the consuls, rais'd and met,
Are at the duke's already: you have been hotly call'd for;
When, being not at your lodging to be found,
The senate hath sent about three several quests
To search you out.

OTHELLO
              'Tis well I am found by you.
I will but spend a word here in the house,
And go with you.   [*Exit.*

CASSIO
            Ancient, what makes he here?

IAGO
Faith, he to-night hath boarded a land carack:
If it prove lawful prize, he's made for ever.

CASSIO
I do not understand.

IAGO
          He's married.

CASSIO
                  To who?

Enter OTHELLO.

IAGO
Marry, to — Come, captain, will you go?

OTHELLO
                    Have with you.

CASSIO

Here comes another troop to seek for you.

IAGO

It is Brabantio: — general, be advised;
He comes to bad intent.

Enter BRABANTIO, RODERIGO, *and* OFFICERS *with
torches and weapons.*

OTHELLO

Holla! stand there!

RODERIGO

Signior, it is the Moor.

BRABANTIO

Down with him, thief!

[*They draw on both sides.*

IAGO

You, Roderigo! come, sir, I am for you.

OTHELLO

Keep up your bright swords, for the dew will rust them. —
Good signior, you shall more command with years
Than with your weapons.

BRABANTIO

O thou foul thief, where hast thou stow'd my daughter?
Damn'd as thou art, thou hast enchanted her;
For I'll refer me to all things of sense,
If she in chains of magic were not bound,
Whether a maid so tender, fair, and happy,
So opposite to marriage that she shunn'd
The wealthy curled darlings of our nation,
Would ever have, t'incur a general mock,
Run from her guardage to the sooty bosom
Of such a thing as thou, — to fear, not to delight.
Judge me the world, if 'tis not gross in sense
That thou hast practis'd on her with foul charms;
Abus'd her delicate youth with drugs or minerals
That weaken motion: — I'll have't disputed on;
'Tis probable, and palpable to thinking.
I therefore apprehend and do attach thee

For an abuser of the world, a practiser
Of arts inhibited and out of warrant. —
Lay hold upon him: if he do resist,
Subdue him at his peril.

OTHELLO

               Hold your hands,
Both you of my inclining, and the rest:
Were it my cue to fight, I should have known it
Without a prompter. — Where will you that I go
To answer this your charge?

BRABANTIO

                     To prison; till fit time
Of law, and course of direct session,
Call thee to answer.

OTHELLO

             What if I do obey?
How may the duke be therewith satisfied,
Whose messengers are here about my side,
Upon some present business of the state
To bring me to him?

FIRST OFFICER

             'Tis true, most worthy signior;
The duke's in council, and your noble self,
I am sure, is sent for.

BRABANTIO

             How! the duke in council!
In this time of the night! — Bring him away;
Mine's not an idle cause: the duke himself,
Or any of my brothers of the state,
Cannot but feel this wrong as 'twere their own;
For if such actions may have passage free,
Bond-slaves and pagans shall our statesmen be.   [*Exeunt.*

SCENE III

A council-chamber.

The DUKE *and* SENATORS *sitting at a table;*
OFFICERS *attending.*

DUKE

There is no composition in these news
That gives them credit.

FIRST SENATOR

                Indeed, they are disproportion'd;
My letters say a hundred and seven galleys.

DUKE

And mine, a hundred and forty.

SECOND SENATOR

                  And mine, two hundred:
But though they jump not on a just account, —
As in these cases, where the aim reports,
'Tis oft with difference, — yet do they all confirm
A Turkish fleet, and bearing up to Cyprus.

DUKE

Nay, it is possible enough to judgement:
I do not so secure me in the error,
But the main article I do approve
In fearful sense.

SAILOR [*within*].

What, ho! what, ho! what, ho!

FIRST OFFICER

A messenger from the galleys.

Enter a SAILOR.

DUKE

                Now, what's the business?

SAILOR

The Turkish preparation makes for Rhodes;
So was I bid report here to the state
By Signior Angelo.

DUKE

How say you by this change?

FIRST SENATOR

             This cannot be,
By no assay of reason: 'tis a pageant,

To keep us in false gaze. When we consider
Th'importancy of Cyprus to the Turk;
And let ourselves again but understand,
That as it more concerns the Turk than Rhodes,
So may he with more facile question bear it,
For that it stands not in such warlike brace,
But altogether lacks th'abilities
That Rhodes is dress'd in: — if we make thought of this,
We must not think the Turk is so unskilful
To leave that latest which concerns him first,
Neglecting an attempt of ease and gain,
To wake and wage a danger profitless.

DUKE

Nay, in all confidence, he's not for Rhodes.

FIRST OFFICER

Here is more news.

Enter a MESSENGER.

MESSENGER

The Ottomites, reverend and gracious,
Steering with due course towards the isle of Rhodes,
Have there injointed them with an after fleet.

FIRST SENATOR

Ay, so I thought. How many, as you guess?

MESSENGER

Of thirty sail: and now they do re-stem
Their backward course, bearing with frank appearance
Their purposes toward Cyprus. — Signior Montano,
Your trusty and most valiant servitor,
With his free duty recommends you thus,
And prays you to believe him.

DUKE

'Tis certain, then, for Cyprus. —
Marcus Luccicos, is not he in town?

FIRST SENATOR

He's now in Florence.

DUKE
Write from us to him; post-post-haste dispatch.

FIRST SENATOR
Here comes Brabantio and the valiant Moor.

Enter BRABANTIO, OTHELLO, IAGO, RODERIGO,
and OFFICERS.

DUKE
Valiant Othello, we must straight employ you
Against the general enemy Ottoman. —
[*to* BRABANTIO] I did not see you; welcome, gentle
    signior;
We lack'd your counsel and your help to-night.

BRABANTIO
So did I yours. Good your Grace, pardon me;
Neither my place, nor aught I heard of business,
Hath rais'd me from my bed; nor doth the general care
Take hold on me; for my particular grief
Is of so flood-gate and o'erbearing nature
That it engluts and swallows other sorrows,
And it is still itself.

DUKE
              Why, what's the matter?

BRABANTIO
My daughter! O, my daughter!

DUKE and SENATOR
                    Dead?

BRABANTIO
Ay, to me;
She is abus'd, stol'n from me, and corrupted
By spells and medicines bought of mountebanks;
For nature so preposterously to err,
Being not deficient, blind, or lame of sense,
Sans witchcraft could not.

DUKE
Whoe'er he be that, in this foul proceeding,
Hath thus beguil'd your daughter of herself,
And you of her, the bloody book of law

You shall yourself read in the bitter letter
After your own sense; yea, though our proper son
Stood in your action.

BRABANTIO

             Humbly I thank your Grace.
Here is the man, this Moor; whom now, it seems,
Your special mandate, for the state-affairs,
Hath hither brought.

DUKE and SENATOR

             We are very sorry for't.

DUKE [*to* OTHELLO].

What, in your own part, can you say to this?

BRABANTIO

Nothing, but this is so.

OTHELLO

Most potent, grave, and reverend signiors,
My very noble and approv'd good masters,
That I have ta'en away this old man's daughter,
It is most true; true, I have married her:
The very head and front of my offending
Hath this extent, no more. Rude am I in my speech,
And little blest with the soft phrase of peace;
For since these arms of mine had seven years' pith,
Till now some nine moons wasted, they have us'd
Their dearest action in the tented field;
And little of this great world can I speak,
More than pertains to feats of broil and battle;
And therefore little shall I grace my cause
In speaking for myself. Yet, by your gracious patience,
I will a round unvarnish'd tale deliver
Of my whole course of love; what drugs, what charms,
What conjuration, and what mighty magic, —
For such proceeding I am charg'd withal, —
I won his daughter.

BRABANTIO

             A maiden never bold;
Of spirit so still and quiet, that her motion

Blush'd at herself; and she — in spite of nature,
Of years, of country, credit, every thing —
To fall in love with what she fear'd to look on!
It is a judgement maim'd and most imperfect,
That will confess perfection so could err
Against all rules of nature; and must be driven
To find out practices of cunning hell,
Why this should be. I therefore vouch again,
That with some mixtures powerful o'er the blood,
Or with some dram conjured to this effect,
He wrought upon her.

DUKE

               To vouch this, is no proof,
Without more wider and more overt test
Than these thin habits and poor likelihoods
Of modern seeming do prefer against him.

FIRST SENATOR

But, Othello, speak:
Did you by indirect and forced courses
Subdue and poison this young maid's affections?
Or came it by request, and such fair question
As soul to soul affordeth?

OTHELLO

             I do beseech you,
Send for the lady to the Sagittary,
And let her speak of me before her father:
If you do find me foul in her report,
The trust, the office, I do hold of you,
Not only take away, but let your sentence
Even fall upon my life.

DUKE

            Fetch Desdemona hither.

OTHELLO

Ancient, conduct them, you best know the place. —
          [*Exeunt* IAGO *and* ATTENDANTS.
And, till she come, as truly as to heaven
I do confess the vices of my blood,

So justly to your grave ears I'll present
How I did thrive in this fair lady's love,
And she in mine.

DUKE

Say it, Othello.

OTHELLO

Her father lov'd me; oft invited me;
Still question'd me the story of my life,
From year to year, — the battles, sieges, fortunes,
That I have pass'd.
I ran it through, even from my boyish days
To the very moment that he bade me tell it:
Wherein I spake of most disastrous chances,
Of moving accidents by flood and field;
Of hair-breadth scapes i'th'imminent deadly breach;
Of being taken by the insolent foe,
And sold to slavery; of my redemption thence,
And portance in my travel's history:
Wherein of antres vast and deserts idle,
Rough quarries, rocks, and hills whose heads touch
    heaven,
It was my hint to speak, — such was the process;
And of the Cannibals that each other eat,
The Anthropophagi, and men whose heads
Do grow beneath their shoulders. This to hear
Would Desdemona seriously incline:
But still the house-affairs would draw her thence;
Which ever as she could with haste dispatch,
She'ld come again, and with a greedy ear
Devour up my discourse: — which I observing,
Took once a pliant hour; and found good means
To draw from her a prayer of earnest heart
That I would all my pilgrimage dilate,
Whereof by parcels she had something heard,
But not intentively: I did consent;
And often did beguile her of her tears,
When I did speak of some distressful stroke

That my youth suffer'd. My story being done,
She gave me for my pains a world of sighs:
She swore, — in faith,'twas strange, 'twas passing
   strange;
'Twas pitiful, 'twas wondrous pitiful:
She wish'd she had not heard it: yet she wish'd
That heaven had made her such a man: she thank'd me;
And bade me, if I had a friend that lov'd her,
I should but teach him how to tell my story,
And that would woo her. Upon this hint I spake:
She lov'd me for the dangers I had pass'd;
And I lov'd her that she did pity them.
This only is the witchcraft I have used: —
Here comes the lady; let her witness it.

Enter DESDEMONA, *with* IAGO *and* ATTENDANTS.

DUKE

I think this tale would win my daughter too. —
Good Brabantio,
Take up this mangled matter at the best:
Men do their broken weapons rather use
Than their bare hands.

BRABANTIO

              I pray you, hear her speak:
If she confess that she was half the wooer,
Destruction on my head, if my bad blame
Light on the man!— Come hither, gentle mistress:
Do you perceive in all this noble company
Where most you owe obedience?

DESDEMONA

              My noble father,
I do perceive here a divided duty:
To you I am bound for life and education;
My life and education both do learn me
How to respect you; you are the lord of duty, —
I am hitherto your daughter: but here's my husband;
And so much duty as my mother show'd
To you, preferring you before her father,

OTHELLO She lov'd me for the dangers I had pass'd.

So much I challenge that I may profess
Due to the Moor my lord.

BRABANTIO

                    God be wi' you! I have done.
Please it your Grace, on to the state-affairs:
I had rather to adopt a child than get it. —
Come hither, Moor:
I here do give thee that with all my heart
Which, but thou hast already, with all my heart
I would keep from thee. — For your sake, jewel,
I am glad at soul I have no other child;
For thy escape would teach me tyranny,
To hang clogs on them. — I have done, my lord.

DUKE

Let me speak like yourself; and lay a sentence,
Which, as a grise or step, may help these lovers
Into your favour.
When remedies are past, the griefs are ended
By seeing the worst, which late on hopes depended.
To mourn a mischief that is past and gone
Is the next way to draw new mischief on.

BRABANTIO I here do give thee that which I would keep from thee.

What cannot be preserv'd when fortune takes,
Patience her injury a mockery makes.
The robb'd that smiles steals something from the thief;
He robs himself that spends a bootless grief.

BRABANTIO
So let the Turk of Cyprus us beguile;
We lose it not, so long as we can smile.
He bears the sentence well that nothing bears
But the free comfort which from thence he hears;
But he bears both the sentence and the sorrow
That to pay grief must of poor patience borrow.

These sentences, to sugar, or to gall,
Being strong on both sides, are equivocal:
But words are words; I never yet did hear
That the bruis'd heart was pierced through the ear. —
I humbly beseech you, proceed to th'affairs of state.

DUKE

The Turk with a most mighty preparation makes for
Cyprus: — Othello, the fortitude of the place is best
known to you; and though we have there a substitute of
most allow'd sufficiency, yet opinion, a sovereign
mistress of effects, throws a more safer voice on you:
you must therefore be content to slubber the gloss of
your new fortunes with this more stubborn and
boisterous expedition.

OTHELLO

The tyrant custom, most grave senators,
Hath made the flinty and steel couch of war
My thrice-driven bed of down: I do agnize
A natural and prompt alacrity
I find in hardness; and do undertake
This present war against the Ottomites.
Most humbly, therefore, bending to your state,
I crave fit disposition for my wife;
Due reference of place and exhibition;
With such accommodation and besort
As levels with her breeding.

DUKE

                    If you please,
Be't at her father's.

BRABANTIO

                    I'll not have it so.

OTHELLO

Nor I.

DESDEMONA

            Nor I; I would not there reside,
To put my father in impatient thoughts
By being in his eye. Most gracious duke,

To my unfolding lend your prosperous ear;
And let me find a charter in your voice,
T'assist my simpleness.

DUKE

What would you, Desdemona?

DESDEMONA

That I did love the Moor to live with him,
My downright violence and storm of fortunes
May trumpet to the world: my heart's subdued
Even to the very quality of my lord:
I saw Othello's visage in his mind;
And to his honours and his valiant parts
Did I my soul and fortunes consecrate.
So that, dear lords, if I be left behind,
A moth of peace, and he go to the war,
The rites for which I love him are bereft me,
And I a heavy interim shall support
By his dear absence. Let me go with him.

OTHELLO

Your voices, lords: beseech you, let her will
Have a free way.
Vouch with me, heaven, I therefore beg it not,
To please the palate of my appetite;
Nor to comply with heat — the young affects
In me defunct — and proper satisfaction;
But to be free and bounteous to her mind:
And heaven defend your good souls, that you think
I will your serious and great business scant
For she is with me: no, when light-wing'd toys
Of feather'd Cupid seel with wanton dullness
My speculative and offic'd instruments,
That my disports corrupt and taint my business,
Let housewives make a skillet of my helm,
And all indign and base adversities
Make head against my estimation!

DUKE

Be it as you shall privately determine,

Either for her stay or going: th'affair cries haste,
And speed must answer it.

FIRST SENATOR

You must away to-night.

OTHELLO

     With all my heart.

DUKE

At nine i' the morning here we'll meet again. —
Othello, leave some officer behind,
And he shall our commission bring to you;
With such things else of quality and respect
As doth import you.

OTHELLO

    So please your Grace, my ancient;
A man he is of honest and trust:
To his conveyance I assign my wife,
With what else needful your good Grace shall think
To be sent after me.

DUKE

    Let it be so. —
Good night to every one. — [*to* BRABANTIO] And,
  noble signior,
If virtue no delighted beauty lack,
Your son-in-law is far more fair than black.

FIRST SENATOR

Adieu, brave Moor: use Desdemona well.

BRABANTIO

Look to her, Moor, if thou hast eyes to see:
She has deceiv'd her father, and may thee.
   [*Exeunt* DUKE, SENATORS, OFFICERS, *etc.*

OTHELLO

My life upon her faith! — Honest Iago,
My Desdemona must I leave to thee:
I prithee, let thy wife attend on her;
And bring them after in the best advantage. —
Come, Desdemona; I have but an hour
Of love, of worldly matters and direction,

To spend with thee: we must obey the time.

[*Exeunt* OTHELLO *and* DESDEMONA.

RODERIGO

Iago, —

IAGO

What say'st thou, noble heart?

RODERIGO

What will I do, think'st thou?

IAGO

Why, go to bed, and sleep.

RODERIGO

I will incontinently drown myself.

IAGO

If thou dost, I shall never love thee after. Why, thou silly
gentleman!

RODERIGO

It is silliness to live when to live is torment; and then
have we a prescription to die when death is our
physician.

IAGO

O villainous! I have look'd upon the world for four times
seven years; and since I could distinguish betwixt a
benefit and an injury, I never found man that knew how
to love himself. Ere I would say, I would drown myself
for the love of a guinea-hen, I would change my
humanity with a baboon.

RODERIGO

What should I do? I confess it is my shame to be so
fond; but it is not in my virtue to amend it.

IAGO

Virtue! a fig! 'tis in ourselves that we are thus or thus.
Our bodies are gardens; to the which our wills are
gardeners: so that if we will plant nettles, or sow lettuce;
set hyssop, and weed-up thyme; supply it with one
gender of herbs, or distract it with many; either to have
it sterile with idleness, or manured with industry; why,

the power and corrigible authority of this lies in our wills. If the balance of our lives had not one scale of reason to poise another of sensuality, the blood and baseness of our natures would conduct us to most preposterous conclusions: but we have reason to cool our raging motions, our carnal stings, our unbitted lusts; whereof I take this that you call love to be a sect or scion.

RODERIGO

It cannot be.

IAGO

It is merely a lust of the blood and a permission of the will. Come, be a man: drown thyself! drown cats and blind puppies. I have profess'd me thy friend, and I confess me knit to thy deserving with cables of perdurable toughness; I could never better stead thee than now. Put money in thy purse; follow thou the wars; defeat thy favour with an usurp'd beard; I say, put money in thy purse. It cannot be that Desdemona should long continue her love to the Moor, — put money in thy purse, — nor he his to her: it was a violent commencement, and thou shalt see an answerable sequestration; — put but money in thy purse. — These Moors are changeable in their wills: — fill thy purse with money: — the food that to him now is as luscious as locusts shall be to him shortly as bitter as coloquintida. She must change for youth; when she is sated with his body, she will find the error of her choice: she must have change, she must: therefore put money in thy purse. — If thou wilt needs damn thyself, do it a more delicate way than drowning. Make all the money thou canst: if sanctimony and a frail vow betwixt an erring barbarian and a supersubtle Venetian be not too hard for my wits and all the tribe of hell, thou shalt enjoy her; therefore make money. A pox of drowning thyself! it is clean out of the way: seek thou rather to be hang'd in compassing thy joy than to be drown'd and go without her.

RODERIGO

Wilt thou be fast to my hopes, if I depend on the issue?

IAGO

Thou art sure of me: — go, make money: — I have told
thee often, and I re-tell thee again and again, I hate the
Moor: my cause is hearted: thine hath no less reason.
Let us be conjunctive in our revenge against him: if thou
canst cuckold him, thou dost thyself a pleasure, me a
sport. There are many events in the womb of time,
which will be deliver'd. Traverse; go; provide thy
money. We will have more of this to-morrow. Adieu.

RODERIGO

Where shall we meet i' the morning?

IAGO

At my lodging.

RODERIGO

I'll be with thee betimes.

IAGO

Go to; farewell. Do you hear, Roderigo?

RODERIGO

What say you?

IAGO

No more of drowning, do you hear?

RODERIGO

I am changed: I'll go sell all my land.

IAGO

Go to; farewell! put money in your purse.

[*Exit* RODERIGO.

Thus do I ever make my fool my purse;
For I mine own gain'd knowledge should profane,
If I would time expend with such a snipe,
But for my sport and profit. I hate the Moor;
And it is thought abroad, that 'twixt my sheets
'Has done my office: I know not if't be true;
But I, for mere suspicion in that kind,
Will do as if for surety. He holds me well;

The better shall my purpose work on him.
Cassio's a proper man: let me see now;
To get his place, and to plume up my will
In double knavery — How, how? — Let's see: —
After some time, to abuse Othello's ear
That he is too familiar with his wife: —
He hath a person, and a smooth dispose,
To be suspected; fram'd to make women false.
The Moor is of a free and open nature,
That thinks men honest that but seem to be so;
And will as tenderly be led by th'nose
As asses are.
I have't; — It is engender'd: — hell and night
Must bring this monstrous birth to the world's light.

[*Exit.*

ACT II

SCENE I

A Seaport town in Cyprus. An open place near the; Quay.

Enter MONTANO *and two* GENTLEMEN.

MONTANO

What from the cape can you discern at sea?

FIRST GENTLEMAN

Nothing at all: it is a high-wrought flood;
I cannot 'twixt the heaven and the main
Descry a sail.

MONTANO

Methinks the wind hath spoke aloud at land;
A fuller blast ne'er shook our battlements:
If it hath ruffian'd so upon the sea,
What ribs of oak, when mountains melt on them,
Can hold the mortise? What shall we hear of this?

SECOND GENTLEMAN

A segregation of the Turkish fleet:
For do but stand upon the foaming shore,
The chidden billow seems to pelt the clouds;
The wind-shak'd surge, with high and monstrous mane,
Seems to cast water on the burning bear,
And quench the guards of th'ever-fixed pole:
I never did like molestation view
On the enchafed flood.

MONTANO

               If that the Turkish fleet
Be not enshelter'd and embay'd, they are drown'd;
It is impossible they bear it out.

Enter a third GENTLEMAN.

THIRD GENTLEMAN

News, lads! our wars are done.
The desperate tempest hath so bang'd the Turks,
That their designment halts: a noble ship of Venice
Hath seen a grievous wrack and sufferance
On most part of their fleet.

MONTANO

How! is this true?

THIRD GENTLEMAN

            The ship is here put in,
A Veronesa; Michael Cassio,
Lieutenant to the warlike Moor Othello,
Is come on shore: the Moor himself's at sea,
And is in full commission here for Cyprus.

MONTANO

I am glad on't; 'tis a worthy governor.

THIRD GENTLEMAN

But this same Cassio, though he speak of comfort
Touching the Turkish loss, yet he looks sadly,
And prays the Moor be safe; for they were parted
With foul and violent tempest.

MONTANO

               Pray heavens he be;

For I have serv'd him, and the man commands
Like a full soldier. Let's to the seaside, ho!
As well to see the vessel that's come in
As to throw out our eyes for brave Othello,
Even till we make the main and th'aerial blue
An indistinct regard.

THIRD GENTLEMAN

     Come, let's do so;
For every minute is expectancy
Of more arrivance.

    Enter CASSIO.

CASSIO

Thanks, you the valiant of this warlike isle,
That so approve the Moor! O, let the heavens
Give him defence against the elements,
For I have lost him on a dangerous sea!

MONTANO

Is he well shipp'd?

CASSIO

His bark is stoutly timber'd, and his pilot
Of very expert and approv'd allowance;
Therefore my hopes, not surfeited to death,
Stand in bold cure.
[*Within*]   A sail, a sail, a sail!

    Enter a fourth GENTLEMAN.

CASSIO

What noise?

FOURTH GENTLEMAN

The town is empty; on the brow o'the sea
Stand ranks of people, and they cry, 'A sail!'

CASSIO

My hopes do shape him for the governor. [*Guns within.*

SECOND GENTLEMAN

They do discharge their shot of courtesy:
Our friends at least.

31

CASSIO

                I pray you, sir, go forth,
And give us truth who 'tis that is arrived.

SECOND GENTLEMAN

  I shall.   *[Exit.*

MONTANO

  But, good lieutenant, is your general wiv'd?

CASSIO

  Most fortunately: he hath achiev'd a maid
That paragons description and wild fame;
One that excels the quirks of blazoning pens,
And in th'essential vesture of creation
Does tire the ingener.

                 Enter second GENTLEMAN.
                     How now! who has put in?

SECOND GENTLEMAN

  'Tis one Iago, ancient to the general.

CASSIO

  'Has had most favourable and happy speed:
Tempests themselves, high seas, and howling winds,
The gutter'd rocks, and congregated sands, —
Traitors ensteep'd to clog the guiltless keel, —
As having sense of beauty, do omit
Their mortal natures, letting go safely by
The divine Desdemona.

MONTANO

                What is she?

CASSIO

  She that I spake of, our great captain's captain,
Left in the conduct of the bold Iago;
Whose footing here anticipates our thoughts
A se'nnight's speed. — Great Jove, Othello guard,
And swell his sail with thine own powerful breath,
That he may bless this bay with his tall ship,
Make love's quick pants in Desdemona's arms,
Give renew'd fire to our extincted spirits,
And bring all Cyprus comfort! — O, behold,

Enter DESDEMONA, EMILIA, IAGO,
RODERIGO, *and* ATTENDANTS.

The riches of the ship is come on shore!
Ye men of Cyprus, let her have your knees. —
Hail to thee, lady! and the grace of heaven
Before, behind thee, and on every hand,
Enwheel thee round!

DESDEMONA

           I thank you, valiant Cassio.
What tidings can you tell me of my lord?

CASSIO

He is not yet arriv'd: nor know I aught
But that he's well, and will be shortly here.

DESDEMONA

O, but I fear — How lost you company?

CASSIO

The great contention of the sea and skies
Parted our fellowship: — but, hark! a sail.
[*Within*] A sail, a sail!   [*Guns within.*

SECOND GENTLEMAN

They give their greeting to the citadel:
This likewise is a friend.

CASSIO

             See for the news. —
                 [*Exit* GENTLEMAN.

Good ancient, you are welcome: — [*to* EMILIA]
    welcome, mistress: —
Let it not gall your patience, good Iago,
That I extend my manners; 'tis my breeding
That gives me this bold show of courtesy.   [*Kissing her.*

IAGO

Sir, would she give you so much of her lips
As of her tongue she oft bestows on me,
You'ld have enough.

DESDEMONA

           Alas, she has no speech.

IAGO

In faith, too much;
I find it still, when I have list to sleep:
Marry, before your ladyship, I grant,
She puts her tongue a little in her heart,
And chides with thinking.

EMILIA

You have little cause to say so.

IAGO

Come on, come on; you are pictures out of doors,
Bells in your parlours, wild-cats in your kitchens,
Saints in your injuries, devils being offended,
Players in your housewifery, and housewives in your beds.

DESDEMONA

O, fie upon thee, slanderer!

IAGO

Nay, it is true, or else I am a Turk:
You rise to play, and go to bed to work.

EMILIA

You shall not write my praise.

IAGO

                No, let me not.

DESDEMONA

What wouldst thou write of me, if thou shouldst praise
me?

IAGO

O gentle lady, do not put me to't;
For I am nothing, if not critical.

DESDEMONA

Come on, assay. — There's one gone to the harbour?

IAGO

Ay, madam.

DESDEMONA

I am not merry; but I do beguile
The thing I am, by seeming otherwise. —
Come, how wouldst thou praise me?

IAGO

I am about it; but, indeed, my invention
Comes from my pate as birdlime does from frize, —
It plucks out brains and all: but my Muse labours,
And thus she is deliver'd.
If she be fair and wise, — fairness and wit,
The one's for use, the other useth it.

DESDEMONA

Well praised! How if she be black and witty?

IAGO

If she be black, and thereto have a wit,
She'll find a white that shall her blackness hit.

DESDEMONA

Worse and worse.

EMILIA

How if fair and foolish?

IAGO

She never yet was foolish that was fair;
For even her folly help'd her to an heir.

DESDEMONA

These are old fond paradoxes to make fools laugh
i'th'alehouse. What miserable praise hast thou for her
that's foul and foolish?

IAGO

There's none so foul, and foolish thereunto,
But does foul pranks which fair and wise ones do.

DESDEMONA

O heavy ignorance! — thou praisest the worst best. But
what praise couldst thou bestow on a deserving woman
indeed, — one that, in the authority of her merit, did
justly put on the vouch of very malice itself?

IAGO

She that was ever fair, and never proud;
Had tongue at will, and yet was never loud;
Never lack'd gold, and yet went never gay;
Fled from her wish, and yet said, 'Now I may';

She that, being anger'd, her revenge being nigh,
Bade her wrong stay, and her displeasure fly;
She that in wisdom never was so frail
To change the cod's head for the salmon's tail;
She that could think, and ne'er disclose her mind;
See suitors following, and not look behind;
She was a wight, if ever such wight were, —

DESDEMONA

To do what?

IAGO

To suckle fools and chronicle small beer.

DESDEMONA

O most lame and impotent conclusion! — Do not learn of
him, Emilia, though he be thy husband. — How say you,
Cassio? is he not a most profane and liberal counsellor?

CASSIO

He speaks home, madam: you may relish him more in
the soldier than in the scholar.

IAGO [*aside*].

He takes her by the palm: ay, well said, whisper: with as
little a web as this will I ensnare as great a fly as Cassio. Ay,
smile upon her, do; I will gyve thee in thine own courtship.
You say true; 'tis so, indeed; if such tricks as these strip you
out of your lieutenantry, it had been better you had not
kiss'd your three fingers so oft, which now again you are
most apt to play the sir in. Very good; well kiss'd! an
excellent courtesy! 'tis so, indeed. Yet again your fingers to
your lips? would they were clyster-pipes for your sake!
[*Trumpet within.*] — The Moor! I know his trumpet.

CASSIO

'Tis truly so.

DESDEMONA

Let's meet him, and receive him.

CASSIO

Lo, where he comes!

Enter OTHELLO *and* ATTENDANTS.

OTHELLO

O my fair warrior!

DESDEMONA

My dear Othello!

OTHELLO

It gives me wonder great as my content
To see you here before me. O my soul's joy!
If after every tempest come such calms,
May the winds blow till they have waken'd death!
And let the labouring bark climb hills of seas
Olympus-high, and duck again as low
As hell's from heaven! If it were now to die,
'Twere now to be most happy; for, I fear,
My soul hath her content so absolute,
That not another comfort like to this
Succeeds in unknown fate.

DESDEMONA

The heavens forbid
But that our loves and comforts should increase,
Even as our days do grow!

OTHELLO

Amen to that, sweet powers!
I cannot speak enough of this content;
It stops me here; it is too much of joy:
And this, and this, the greatest discords be   [*Kissing her.*
That e'er our hearts shall make!

IAGO [*aside*].

O, you are well tun'd now!
But I'll set down the pegs that make this music,
As honest as I am.

OTHELLO

Come, let us to the castle. —
News, friends; our wars are done, the Turks are
    drown'd.
How does my old acquaintance of this isle? —
Honey, you shall be well desired in Cyprus;
I have found great love amongst them. O my sweet,

I prattle out of fashion, and I dote
In mine own comforts. — I prithee, good Iago,
Go to the bay and disembark my coffers:
Bring thou the master to the citadel;
He is a good one, and his worthiness
Does challenge much respect. — Come, Desdemona,
Once more well met at Cyprus.

[*Exeunt* OTHELLO, DESDEMONA, *and*
ATTENDANTS.

IAGO

Do thou meet me presently at the harbour. Come
hither. If thou be'st valiant, — as, they say, base men
being in love have then a nobility in their natures more
than is native to them, — list me. The lieutenant to-
night watches on the court-of-guard: — first, I must tell
thee this — Desdemona is directly in love with him.

RODERIGO

With him! why, 'tis not possible.

IAGO

Lay thy finger thus, and let thy soul be instructed. Mark
me with what violence she first loved the Moor, but for
bragging, and telling her fantastical lies: and will she love
him still for prating? let not thy discreet heart think it.
Her eye must be fed; and what delight shall she have to
look on the devil? When the blood is made dull with the
act of sport, there should be — again to inflame it, and to
give satiety a fresh appetite — loveliness in favour,
sympathy in years, manners, and beauties; all which the
Moor is defective in: now, for want of these required
conveniences, her delicate tenderness will find itself
abused, begin to heave the gorge, disrelish and abhor the
Moor; very nature will instruct her in it, and compel her
to some second choice. Now, sir, this granted, — as it is a
most pregnant and unforced position, — who stands so
eminent in the degree of this fortune as Cassio does? a
knave very voluble; no further conscionable than in
putting on the mere form of civil and humane seeming,

for the better compassing of his salt and most hidden
loose affection? Why, none; why, none: a slipper and
subtle knave; a finder of occasions; that has an eye can
stamp and counterfeit advantages, though true advantage
never present itself: a devilish knave! Besides, the knave is
handsome, young, and hath all those requisites in him
that folly and green minds look after: a pestilent complete
knave; and the woman hath found him already.

RODERIGO

I cannot believe that in her; she's full of most blest
condition.

IAGO

Blest fig's-end! the wine she drinks is made of grapes: if
she had been blest, she would never have loved the
Moor: blest pudding! Didst thou not see her paddle with
the palm of his hand? didst not mark that?

RODERIGO

Yes, that I did; but that was but courtesy.

IAGO

Lechery, by this hand; an index and obscure prologue to
the history of lust and foul thoughts. They met so near
with their lips, that their breaths embraced together.
Villainous thoughts, Roderigo! when these mutualities so
marshal the way, hard at hand comes the master and main
exercise, the incorporate conclusion: pish! — But, sir, be
you ruled by me: I have brought you from Venice. Watch
you to-night; for the command, I'll lay't upon you: Cassio
knows you not: — I'll not be far from you: do you find
some occasion to anger Cassio, either by speaking too
loud, or tainting his discipline; or from what other course
you please, which the time shall more favourably minister.

RODERIGO

Well.

IAGO

Sir, he is rash, and very sudden in choler, and haply may
strike at you: provoke him, that he may; for even out of
that will I cause these of Cyprus to mutiny; whose

qualification shall come into no true taste again but by
the displanting of Cassio. So shall you have a shorter
journey to your desires, by the means I shall then have
to prefer them; and the impediment most profitably
removed, without the which there were no expectation
of our prosperity.

RODERIGO

I will do this, if I can bring it to any opportunity.

IAGO

I warrant thee. Meet me by and by at the citadel:
I must fetch his necessaries ashore. Farewell.

RODERIGO

Adieu.   [*Exit.*

IAGO

That Cassio loves her, I do well believe it;
That she loves him, 'tis apt, and of great credit:
The Moor — howbeit that I endure him not —
Is of a constant, loving, noble nature;
And I dare think he'll prove to Desdemona
A most dear husband. Now, I do love her too;
Not out of absolute lust, — though peradventure
I stand accountant for as great a sin, —
But partly led to diet my revenge,
For that I do suspect the lusty Moor
Hath leapt into my seat: the thought whereof
Doth, like a poisonous mineral, gnaw my inwards;
And nothing can or shall content my soul
Till I am even'd with him, wife for wife;
Or failing so, yet that I put the Moor
At least into a jealousy so strong
That judgement cannot cure. Which thing to do,
If this poor trash of Venice, whom I trash
For his quick hunting, stand the putting on,
I'll have our Michael Cassio on the hip;
Abuse him to the Moor in the rank garb, —
For I fear Cassio with my night-cap too;
Make the Moor thank me, love me, and reward me,

For making him egregiously an ass,
And practising upon his peace and quiet
Even to madness. 'Tis here, but yet confused:
Knavery's plain face is never seen till used.   [*Exit.*

SCENE II

A street.

Enter OTHELLO'S HERALD *with a proclamation;*
PEOPLE *following.*

HERALD

It is Othello's pleasure, our noble and valiant general,
that, upon certain tidings now arrived, importing the
mere perdition of the Turkish fleet, every man put
himself into triumph; some to dance, some to make
bonfires, each man to what sport and revels his
addiction leads him: for, besides these beneficial news, it
is the celebration of his nuptial: — so much was his
pleasure should be proclaim'd. All offices are open; and
there is full liberty of feasting from this present hour of
five till the bell have told eleven. Heaven bless the isle of
Cyprus and our noble general Othello!   [*Exeunt.*

SCENE III

A hall in the castle.

Enter OTHELLO, DESDEMONA, CASSIO,
and ATTENDANTS.

OTHELLO

Good Michael, look you to the guard to-night:
Let's teach ourselves that honourable stop,
Not to outsport discretion.

CASSIO

Iago hath direction what to do;
But, notwithstanding, with my personal eye
Will I look to't.

41

OTHELLO

Iago is most honest.
Michael, good night: to-morrow with your earliest
Let me have speech with you. — [*to* DESDEMONA]
Come, my dear love, —
The purchase made, the fruits are to ensue;
That profit's yet to come 'twixt me and you. —
Good night.

[*Exeunt* OTHELLO, DESDEMONA,
and ATTENDANTS.

Enter IAGO.

CASSIO

Welcome, Iago; we must to the watch.

IAGO

Not this hour, lieutenant; 'tis not yet ten o'the clock.
Our general cast us thus early for the love of his
Desdemona; who let us not therefore blame; he hath not
yet made wanton the night with her; and she is sport for
Jove.

CASSIO

She's a most exquisite lady.

IAGO

And, I'll warrant her, full of game.

CASSIO

Indeed, she's a most fresh and delicate creature.

IAGO

What an eye she has! methinks it sounds a parley to
provocation.

CASSIO

An inviting eye; and yet methinks right modest.

IAGO

And when she speaks, is it not an alarum to love?

CASSIO

She is, indeed, perfection.

42

IAGO

Well, happiness to their sheets! Come, lieutenant, I have
a stoop of wine; and here without are a brace of Cyprus
gallants that would fain have a measure to the health of
black Othello.

CASSIO

Not to-night, good Iago: I have very poor and unhappy
brains for drinking: I could well wish courtesy would
invent some other custom of entertainment.

IAGO

O, they are our friends; but one cup: I'll drink for you.

CASSIO

I have drunk but one cup to-night, and that was craftily
qualified too, and, behold, what innovation it makes
here: I am unfortunate in the infirmity, and dare not
task my weakness with any more.

IAGO

What, man! 'tis a night of revels: the gallants desire it.

CASSIO

Where are they?

IAGO

Here at the door; I pray you, call them in.

CASSIO

I'll do't; but it dislikes me.   [*Exit.*

IAGO

If I can fasten but one cup upon him,
With that which he hath drunk to-night already,
He'll be as full of quarrel and offence
As my young mistress' dog. Now, my sick fool
    Roderigo,
Whom love hath turn'd almost the wrong side out,
To Desdemona hath to-night caroused
Potations pottle-deep; and he's to watch:
Three lads of Cyprus — noble swelling spirits,
That hold their honours in a wary distance,
The very elements of this warlike isle —
Have I to-night fluster'd with flowing cups,

And they watch too. Now, 'mongst this flock of
   drunkards
Am I to put our Cassio in some action
That may offend the isle: — but here they come:
If consequence do but approve my dream,
My boat sails freely, both with wind and stream.

   Enter CASSIO, MONTANO *and* GENTLEMEN;
      SERVANTS *following with wine.*

CASSIO

'Fore God, they have given me a rouse already.

MONTANO

Good faith, a little one; not past a pint, as I am a soldier.

IAGO

Some wine, ho!   [*Sings.*

    And let me the canakin clink, clink;
    And let me the canakin clink;
       A soldier's a man;
       A life's but a span;
    Why, then, let a soldier drink.

Some wine, boys!

CASSIO

'Fore God, an excellent song.

IAGO

I learn'd it in England, where, indeed, they are most
potent in potting: your Dane, your German, and your
swag-bellied Hollander, — Drink, ho! — are nothing to
your English.

CASSIO

Is your Englishman so expert in his drinking?

IAGO

Why, he drinks you, with facility, your Dane dead
drunk; he sweats not to overthrow your Almain; he gives
your Hollander a vomit, ere the next pottle can be fill'd.

CASSIO

To the health of our general!

CASIO To the health of our general!

MONTANO
 I am for it, lieutenant; and I'll do you justice.
IAGO
 O sweet England!   [*Sings.*
          King Stephen was a worthy peer,
               His breeches cost him but a crown;
          He held them sixpence all too dear,
               With that he call'd the tailor lown.

          He was a wight of high renown,
               And thou art but of low degree:
          'Tis pride that pulls the country down;
               Then take thine auld cloak about thee.
 Some wine, ho!
CASSIO
 Why, this is a more exquisite song than the other.
IAGO
 Will you hear't again?

45

CASSIO

No; for I hold him to be unworthy of his place that does those things. — Well, — God's above all; and there be souls must be saved, and there be souls must not be saved.

IAGO

It's true, good lieutenant.

CASSIO

For mine own part, — no offence to the general, nor any man of quality, — I hope to be saved.

IAGO

And so do I too, lieutenant.

CASSIO

Ay, but, by your leave, not before me; the lieutenant is to be saved before the ancient. Let's have no more of this; let's to our affairs. — God forgive us our sins! — Gentlemen, let's look to our business. Do not think, gentlemen, I am drunk: this is my ancient; — This is my right hand, and this is my left: — I am not drunk now; I can stand well enough, and speak well enough.

ALL

Excellent well.

CASSIO

Why, very well, then; you must not think, then, that I am drunk. [*Exit.*

MONTANO

To the platform, masters; come, let's set the watch.

IAGO

You see this fellow that is gone before; —
He is a soldier fit to stand by Cæsar
And give direction: and do but see his vice;
'Tis to his virtue a just equinox,
The one as long as th'other: 'tis pity of him.
I fear the trust Othello puts him in,
On some odd time of his infirmity,
Will shake this island.

MONTANO
                But is he often thus?

IAGO
'Tis evermore the prologue to his sleep:
He'll watch the horologe a double set,
If drink rock not his cradle.

MONTANO
                It were well
The general were put in mind of it.
Perhaps he sees it not; or his good nature
Prizes the virtue that appears in Cassio,
And looks not on his evils: is not this true?

              Enter RODERIGO.

IAGO [*aside to* RODERIGO].
How now, Roderigo!
I pray you, after the lieutenant; go.   [*Exit* RODERIGO.

MONTANO
And 'tis great pity that the noble Moor
Should hazard such a place as his own second
With one of an ingraft infirmity:
It were an honest action to say
So to the Moor.

IAGO
              Not I, for this fair island:
I do love Cassio well; and would do much
To cure him of this evil — But, hark! what noise?
            [*Cry within,* — 'Help! help!'

    Enter CASSIO, *driving in* RODERIGO.

CASSIO
Zounds, you rogue! you rascal!

MONTANO
What's the matter, lieutenant?

CASSIO
A knave teach me my duty! but I'll beat the knave into a
twiggen bottle.

RODERIGO
Beat me!

CASSIO
Dost thou prate, rogue?   [*Striking* RODERIGO.

MONTANO
Nay, good lieutenant; I pray you, sir, hold your hand.

CASSIO
Let me go, sir, or I'll knock you o'er the mazard.

MONTANO
Come, come, you're drunk.

CASSIO
Drunk!   [*They fight.*

IAGO [*aside to* RODERIGO].
Away, I say, go out; and cry a mutiny!
                                        [*Exit* RODERIGO.
Nay, good lieutenant, — God's will, gentlemen; —
Help, ho! — Lieutenant, — sir, — Montano, — sir; —
Help, masters! — Here's a goodly watch indeed! [*Bell rings.*
Who's that which rings the bell? — Diablo, ho!
The town will rise: God's will, lieutenant, hold;
You will be sham'd for ever.

        Enter OTHELLO *and* ATTENDANTS.

OTHELLO
                    What is the matter here?

MONTANO
Zounds, I bleed still; I am hurt to the death.   [*Faints.*

OTHELLO
Hold, for your lives!

IAGO
Hold, ho! Lieutenant, — sir, — Montano, —
    gentlemen, —
Have you forgot all sense of place and duty?
Hold! the general speaks to you; hold, hold, for shame!

OTHELLO
Why, how now, ho! from whence ariseth this?
Are we turn'd Turks, and to ourselves do that
Which heaven hath forbid the Ottomites?
For Christian shame, put by this barbarous brawl:

He that stirs next to carve for his own rage,
Holds his soul light; he dies upon his motion. —
Silence that dreadful bell! it frights the isle
From her propriety. — What is the matter, masters? —
Honest Iago, that look'st dead with grieving,
Speak, who began this? on thy love, I charge thee.

IAGO

I do not know: — friends all but now, even now,
In quarter, and in terms like bride and groom
Devesting them for bed; and then, but now —
As if some planet had unwitted men —
Swords out, and tilting one at other's breast,
In opposition bloody. I cannot speak
Any beginning to this peevish odds;
And would in action glorious I had lost
Those legs that brought me to a part of it!

OTHELLO

How comes it, Michael, you are thus forgot?

CASSIO

I pray you, pardon me; I cannot speak.

OTHELLO

Worthy Montano, you were wont be civil;
The gravity and stillness of your youth
The world hath noted, and your name is great
In mouths of wisest censure: what's the matter,
That you unlace your reputation thus,
And spend your rich opinion for the name
Of a night-brawler? give me answer to it.

MONTANO

Worthy Othello, I am hurt to danger:
Your officer, Iago, can inform you —
While I spare speech, which something now offends me —
Of all that I do know: nor know I aught
By me that's said or done amiss this night;
Unless self-charity be sometimes a vice,
And to defend ourselves it be a sin

When violence assails us.

OTHELLO
                    Now by heaven,
My blood begins my safer guides to rule;
And passion, having my best judgement collied,
Assays to lead the way: — if I once stir,
Or do but lift this arm, the best of you
Shall sink in my rebuke. Give me to know
How this foul rout began, who set it on;
And he that is approv'd in this offence,
Though he had twinn'd with me, both at a birth,
Shall lose me. — What! in a town of war,
Yet wild, the people's hearts brimful of fear,
To manage private and domestic quarrel,
In night, and on the court and guard of safety!
'Tis monstrous — Iago, who began't?

MONTANO
If partially affin'd, or leagued in office,
Thou dost deliver more or less than truth,
Thou art no soldier.

IAGO
                    Touch me not so near:
I had rather have this tongue cut from my mouth
Than it should do offence to Michael Cassio;
Yet, I persuade myself, to speak the truth
Shall nothing wrong him. — Thus it is, general.
Montano and myself being in speech,
There comes a fellow crying out for help;
And Cassio following him with determin'd sword
To execute upon him. Sir, this gentleman
Steps in to Cassio, and entreats his pause:
Myself the crying fellow did pursue,
Lest by his clamour — as it so fell out —
The town might fall in fright: he, swift of foot,
Outran my purpose; and I return'd the rather
For that I heard the clink and fall of swords,
And Cassio high in oath; which till to-night

I ne'er might say before. When I came back, —
For this was brief, — I found them close together,
At blow and thrust; even as again they were
When you yourself did part them.
More of this matter cannot I report: —
But men are men; the best sometimes forget: —
Though Cassio did some little wrong to him, —
As men in rage strike those that wish them best, —
Yet, surely, Cassio, I believe, received
From him that fled some strange indignity,
Which patience could not pass.

OTHELLO

                I know, Iago,
Thy honesty and love doth mince this matter,
Making it light to Cassio. — Cassio, I love thee;
But never more be officer of mine. —

        Enter DESDEMONA, *attended.*

Look, if my gentle love be not rais'd up! —
I'll make thee an example.

DESDEMONA

              What's the matter?

OTHELLO

All's well now, sweeting; come away to bed. —
Sir, for your hurts, myself will be your surgeon:
Lead him off.   [*Exeunt some with* MONTANO.
Iago, look with care about the town,
And silence those whom this vile brawl distracted. —
Come, Desdemona: 'tis the soldiers' life
To have their balmy slumbers wak'd with strife.
        [*Exeunt all but* IAGO *and* CASSIO.

IAGO

What, are you hurt, lieutenant?

CASSIO

Ay, past all surgery.

IAGO

Marry, heaven forbid!

IAGO What, are you hurt, lieutenant?

CASSIO

Reputation, reputation, reputation! O, I have lost my
reputation! I have lost the immortal part of myself, and
what remains is bestial. — My reputation, Iago, my
reputation!

IAGO

As I am an honest man, I thought you had received
some bodily wound; there is more sense in that than
in reputation. Reputation is an idle and most false
imposition; oft got without merit, and lost without
deserving: you have lost no reputation at all, unless
you repute yourself such a loser. What, man! there are
ways to recover the general again: you are but now
cast in his mood, a punishment more in policy than in
malice, even so as one would beat his offenceless dog
to affright an imperious lion: sue to him again, and
he's yours.

CASSIO

I will rather sue to be despised than to deceive so good a
commander with so slight, so drunken, and so indiscreet
an officer. Drunk? and speak parrot? and squabble?
swagger? swear? and discourse fustian with one's own
shadow? — O thou invisible spirit of wine, if thou hast
no name to be known by, let us call thee devil!

IAGO

What was he that you follow'd with your sword?
What had he done to you?

CASSIO

I know not.

IAGO

Is't possible?

CASSIO

I remember a mass of things, but nothing distinctly; a
quarrel, but nothing wherefore. — O God, that men
should put an enemy in their mouths to steal away their
brains! that we should, with joy, pleasance, revel, and
applause, transform ourselves into beasts!

IAGO

Why, but you are now well enough: how came you thus
recover'd?

CASSIO

It hath pleased the devil drunkenness to give place to the
devil wrath: one unperfectness shows me another, to
make me frankly despise myself.

IAGO

Come, you are too severe a moraler: as the time, the
place, and the condition of this country stands, I could
heartily wish this had not befall'n; but, since it is as it is,
mend it for your own good.

CASSIO

I will ask him for my place again, — he shall tell me I
am a drunkard! Had I as many mouths as Hydra, such
an answer would stop them all. To be now a sensible
man, by and by a fool, and presently a beast! O strange!

— Every inordinate cup is unblest, and the ingredient is a devil.

IAGO

Come, come, good wine is a good familiar creature, if it be well used: exclaim no more against it. And, good lieutenant, I think you think I love you.

CASSIO

I have well approved it, sir. — I drunk!

IAGO

You or any man living may be drunk at a time, man. I'll tell you what you shall do. Our general's wife is now the general; — I may say so in this respect, for that he hath devoted and given up himself to the contemplation, mark, and denotement of her parts and graces: — confess yourself freely to her; importune her help to put you in your place again: she is of so free, so kind, so apt, so blessed a disposition, she holds it a vice in her goodness not to do more than she is requested: this broken joint between you and her husband entreat her to splinter; and, my fortunes against any lay worth naming, this crack of your love shall grow stronger than it was before.

CASSIO

You advise me well.

IAGO

I protest, in the sincerity of love and honest kindness.

CASSIO

I think it freely; and betimes in the morning I will beseech the virtuous Desdemona to undertake for me: I am desperate of my fortunes if they check me here.

IAGO

You are in the right. Good night, lieutenant; I must to the watch.

CASSIO

Good night, honest Iago.   [*Exit.*

IAGO

And what's he, then, that says I play the villain?

When this advice is free I give and honest,
Probal to thinking, and, indeed, the course
To win the Moor again? For 'tis most easy
Th'inclining Desdemona to subdue
In any honest suit: she's fram'd as fruitful
As the free elements. And then for her
To win the Moor, — were't to renounce his baptism,
All seals and symbols of redeemed sin,
His soul is so enfetter'd to her love,
That she may make, unmake, do what she list,
Even as her appetite shall play the god
With his weak function. How am I, then, a villain
To counsel Cassio to this parallel course,
Directly to his good? Divinity of hell!
When devils will the blackest sins put on,
They do suggest at first with heavenly shows,
As I do now: for whiles this honest fool
Plies Desdemona to repair his fortunes,
And she for him pleads strongly to the Moor,
I'll pour this pestilence into his ear, —
That she repeals him for her body's lust;
And by how much she strives to do him good,
She shall undo her credit with the Moor.
So will I turn her virtue into pitch;
And out of her own goodness make the net
That shall enmesh them all.

Enter RODERIGO.

How now, Roderigo!

RODERIGO

I do follow here in the chase, not like a hound that
hunts, but one that fills up the cry. My money is almost
spent; I have been to-night exceedingly well cudgell'd;
and I think the issue will be — I shall have so much
experience for my pains; and so, with no money at all,
and a little more wit, return again to Venice.

IAGO

How poor are they that have not patience!

What wound did ever heal but by degrees?
Thou know'st we work by wit, and not by witchcraft;
And wit depends on dilatory time.
Does't not go well? Cassio hath beaten thee,
And thou, by that small hurt, hast cashier'd Cassio:
Though other things grow fair against the sun,
Yet fruits that blossom first will first be ripe:
Content thyself awhile. — By th'mass, 'tis morning;
Pleasure and action make the hours seem short. —
Retire thee; go where thou art billeted:
Away, I say; thou shalt know more hereafter:
Nay, get thee gone. [*Exit* RODERIGO.] Two things are
   to be done, —
My wife must move for Cassio to her mistress;
I'll set her on;
Myself the while to draw the Moor apart,
And bring him jump when he may Cassio find
Soliciting his wife: — ay, that's the way;
Dull not device by coldness and delay.   [*Exit.*

ACT III

SCENE I

Cyprus. Before the castle.

Enter CASSIO *and some* MUSICIANS.

CASSIO

Masters, play here, — I will content your pains, —
Something that's brief; and bid 'Good morrow, general.'
                        [*Music.*

Enter CLOWN.

CLOWN

Why, masters, have your instruments been in
Naples, that they speak i'th'nose thus?

FIRST MUSICIAN
  How, sir, how!

CLOWN
  Are these, I pray you, wind-instruments?

FIRST MUSICIAN
  Ay, marry, are they, sir.

CLOWN
  O, thereby hangs a tail.

FIRST MUSICIAN
  Whereby hangs a tale, sir?

CLOWN
  Marry, sir, by many a wind-instrument that I know.
  But, masters, here's money for you: and the general so
  likes your music, that he desires you, of all loves, to
  make no more noise with it.

FIRST MUSICIAN
  Well, sir, we will not.

CLOWN
  If you have any music that may not be heard, to't again:
  but, as they say, to hear music the general does not
  greatly care.

FIRST MUSICIAN
  We have none such, sir.

CLOWN
  Then put up your pipes in your bag, for I'll away: go;
  vanish into air; away!   [*Exeunt* MUSICIANS.

CASSIO
  Dost thou hear, my honest friend?

CLOWN
  No, I hear not your honest friend; I hear you.

CASSIO
  Prithee, keep up thy quillets. There's a poor piece of
  gold for thee: if the gentlewoman that attends the
  general's wife be stirring, tell her there's one Cassio
  entreats her a little favour of speech: wilt thou do this?

CLOWN

She is stirring, sir: if she will stir hither, I shall seem to
notify unto her.

CASSIO

Do, good my friend.   [*Exit* CLOWN.

     Enter IAGO.
  In happy time, Iago.

IAGO

You have not been a-bed, then?

CASSIO

Why, no; the day had broke
Before we parted. I have made bold, Iago,
To send in to your wife: my suit to her
Is, that she will to virtuous Desdemona
Procure me some access.

IAGO

      I'll send her to you presently;
And I'll devise a mean to draw the Moor
Out of the way, that your converse and business
May be more free.

CASSIO

I humbly thank you for't. [*Exit* IAGO.] I never knew
A Florentine more kind and honest.

    Enter EMILIA.

EMILIA

Good morrow, good Lieutenant: I am sorry
For your displeasure; but all will sure be well.
The general and his wife are talking of it;
And she speaks for you stoutly: the Moor replies,
That he you hurt is of great fame in Cyprus
And great affinity, and that in wholesome wisdom
He might not but refuse you; but he protests he loves
 you,
And needs no other suitor but his likings
To take the safest occasion by the front
To bring you in again.

CASSIO

               Yet, I beseech you, —
If you think fit, or that it may be done, —
Give me advantage of some brief discourse
With Desdemona alone.

EMILIA

               Pray you, come in:
I will bestow you where you shall have time
To speak your bosom freely.

CASSIO

             I am much bound to you.   [*Exeunt.*

SCENE II

A room in the castle.

Enter OTHELLO, IAGO, *and* GENTLEMEN.

OTHELLO

These letters give, Iago, to the pilot;
And, by him, do my duties to the senate:
That done, I will be walking on the works;
Repair there to me.

IAGO

             Well, my good lord, I'll do't.

OTHELLO

This fortification, gentlemen, — shall we see't?

GENTLEMAN

We'll wait upon your lordship.   [*Exeunt.*

SCENE III

The garden of the castle.

Enter DESDEMONA, CASSIO, *and* EMILIA.

DESDEMONA

Be thou assured, good Cassio, I will do
All my abilities in thy behalf.

EMILIA

Good madam, do: I warrant it grieves my husband,
As if the case were his.

DESDEMONA

O, that's an honest fellow. — Do not doubt, Cassio,
But I will have my lord and you again
As friendly as you were.

CASSIO

               Bounteous madam,
Whatever shall become of Michael Cassio,
He's never anything but your true servant.

DESDEMONA

I know't, — I thank you. You do love my lord:
You have known him long; and be you well assured
He shall in strangeness stand no further off
Than in a polite distance.

CASSIO

               Ay, but, lady,
That policy may either last so long,
Or feed upon such nice and waterish diet,
Or breed itself so out of circumstance,
That, I being absent, and my place supplied,
My general will forget my love and service.

DESDEMONA

Do not doubt that; before Emilia here
I give thee warrant of thy place: assure thee,
If I do vow a friendship, I'll perform it
To the last article: my lord shall never rest;
I'll watch him tame, and talk him out of patience;
His bed shall seem a school, his board a shrift;
I'll intermingle every thing he does
With Cassio's suit: therefore be merry, Cassio;
For thy solicitor shall rather die
Than give thy cause away.

EMILIA

Madam, here comes my lord.

CASSIO
Madam, I'll take my leave.

DESDEMONA
Why, stay, and hear me speak.

CASSIO
Madam, not now: I am very ill at ease,
Unfit for mine own purposes.

DESDEMONA
Well, do your discretion.   [*Exit* CASSIO.
          Enter OTHELLO *and* IAGO.

IAGO
Ha! I like not that.

OTHELLO
                    What dost thou say?

IAGO
Nothing, my lord: or if — I know not what.

CASIO Madam, I'll take my leave.

OTHELLO

Was not that Cassio parted from my wife?

IAGO

Cassio, my lord! No, sure, I cannot think it,
That he would steal away so guilty-like,
Seeing you coming.

OTHELLO

          I do believe 'twas he.

DESDEMONA

How now, my lord!
I have been talking with a suitor here,
A man that languishes in your displeasure.

OTHELLO

Who is't you mean?

DESDEMONA

Why, your lieutenant, Cassio. Good my lord,
If I have any grace or power to move you,
His present reconciliation take;
For if he be not one that truly loves you,
That errs in ignorance, and not in cunning,
I have no judgement in an honest face:
I prithee, call him back.

OTHELLO

          Went he hence now?

DESDEMONA

Ay, sooth; so humbled,
That he hath left part of his grief with me,
To suffer with him. Good love, call him back.

OTHELLO

Not now, sweet Desdemona; some other time.

DESDEMONA

But shall't be shortly?

OTHELLO

          The sooner, sweet, for you.

DESDEMONA

Shall't be to-night at supper?

OTHELLO

               No, not to-night.

DESDEMONA

 To-morrow dinner, then?

OTHELLO

                 I shall not dine at home;
I meet the captains at the citadel.

DESDEMONA

 Why, then, to-morrow night; or Tuesday morn;
On Tuesday morn, or night; on Wednesday morn: —
I prithee, name the time; but let it not
Exceed three days: in faith, he's penitent;
And yet his trespass, in our common reason, —
Save that, they say, the wars must make examples
Out of their best, — is not almost a fault
T'incur a private check. When shall he come?
Tell me, Othello: I wonder in my soul,
What you would ask me, that I should deny,
Or stand so mammering on. What! Michael Cassio,
That came a-wooing with you; and so many a time,
When I have spoke of you dispraisingly,
Hath ta'en your part; to have so much to do
To bring him in! Trust me, I could do much —

OTHELLO

 Prithee, no more: let him come when he will;
I will deny thee nothing.

DESDEMONA

            Why, this is not a boon;
'Tis as I should entreat you wear your gloves,
Or feed on nourishing dishes, or keep you warm,
Or sue to you to do a peculiar profit
To your own person: nay, when I have a suit
Wherein I mean to touch your love indeed,
It shall be full of poise and difficult weight,
And fearful to be granted.

OTHELLO

              I will deny thee nothing:

Whereon, I do beseech thee, grant me this,
To leave me but a little to myself.

DESDEMONA

Shall I deny you? no: farewell, my lord.

OTHELLO

Farewell, my Desdemona: I'll come to thee straight.

DESDEMONA

Emilia, come. — Be as your fancies teach you;
Whate'er you be, I am obedient.   [*Exit, with* EMILIA.

OTHELLO

Excellent wretch! Perdition catch my soul,
But I do love thee! and when I love thee not,
Chaos is come again.

IAGO

My noble lord, —

OTHELLO

             What does thou say, Iago?

IAGO

Did Michael Cassio, when you woo'd my lady,
Know of your love?

OTHELLO

He did, from first to last: why dost thou ask?

IAGO

But for a satisfaction of my thought;
No further harm.

OTHELLO

             Why of thy thought, Iago?

IAGO

I did not think he had been acquainted with her.

OTHELLO

O, yes; and went between us very oft.

IAGO

Indeed!

OTHELLO

Indeed! ay, indeed: — discern'st thou aught in that?
Is he not honest?

IAGO

Honest, my lord!

OTHELLO

Honest! ay, honest.

IAGO

My lord, for aught I know.

OTHELLO

What dost thou think?

IAGO

Think, my lord!

OTHELLO

Think, my lord!

By heaven, he echoes me,
As if there were some monster in his thought
Too hideous to be shown. — Thou dost mean
    something:
I heard thee say even now, thou likedst not that,
When Cassio left my wife: what didst not like?
And when I told thee he was of my counsel
In my whole course of wooing, thou criedst 'Indeed!'
And didst contract and purse thy brow together,
As if thou then hadst shut up in thy brain
Some horrible conceit: if thou dost love me,
Show me thy thought.

IAGO

My lord, you know I love you.

OTHELLO

I think thou dost;
And, for I know thou'rt full of love and honesty,
And weigh'st thy words before thou givest them breath,
Therefore these stops of thine fright me the more:
For such things in a false disloyal knave
Are tricks of custom; but in a man that's just
They're close delations, working from the heart,
That passion cannot rule.

IAGO

For Michael Cassio,

I dare be sworn I think that he is honest.

OTHELLO

I think so too.

IAGO

    Men should be what they seem;
Or those that be not, would they might seem none!

OTHELLO

Certain, men should be what they seem.

IAGO

Why, then, I think Cassio's an honest man.

OTHELLO

Nay, yet there's more in this:
I prithee, speak to me as to thy thinkings,
As thou dost ruminate; and give thy worst of thoughts
The worst of words.

IAGO

    Good my lord, pardon me:
Though I am bound to every act of duty,
I am not bound to that all slaves are free to.
Utter my thoughts? Why, say they are vile and false, —
As where's that palace whereinto foul things
Sometimes intrude not? who has a breast so pure,
But some uncleanly apprehensions
Keep leets and law-days and in session sit
With meditations lawful?

OTHELLO

Thou dost conspire against thy friend, Iago,
If thou but think'st him wrong'd, and makest his ear
A stranger to thy thoughts.

IAGO

    I do beseech you —
Though I perchance am vicious in my guess,
As, I confess, it is my nature's plague
To spy into abuses, and oft my jealousy
Shapes faults that are not — that your wisdom yet,
From one that so imperfectly conceits,
Would take no notice; nor build yourself a trouble

Out of his scattering and unsure observance: —
It were not for your quiet nor your good,
Nor for my manhood, honesty, or wisdom,
To let you know my thoughts.

OTHELLO

What dost thou mean?

IAGO

Good name in man and woman, dear my lord,
Is the immediate jewel of their souls:
Who steals my purse steals trash; 'tis something,
   nothing;
'Twas mine, 'tis his, and has been slave to thousands;
But he that filches from me my good name
Robs me of that which not enriches him,
And makes me poor indeed.

OTHELLO

By heaven, I'll know thy thoughts!

IAGO

You cannot, if my heart were in your hand;
Nor shall not, whilst 'tis in my custody.

OTHELLO

Ha!

IAGO

O, beware, my lord, of jealousy;
It is the green-eyed monster, which doth mock
The meat it feeds on: that cuckold lives in bliss
Who, certain of his fate, loves not his wronger;
But, O, what damned minutes tells he o'er
Who dotes, yet doubts, suspects, yet strongly loves!

OTHELLO

O misery!

IAGO

Poor and content is rich, and rich enough;
But riches fineless is as poor as winter
To him that ever fears he shall be poor: —
Good heaven, the souls of all my tribe defend
From jealousy!

OTHELLO

     Why, why is this?
Think'st thou I'ld make a life of jealousy,
To follow still the changes of the moon
With fresh suspicions? No; to be once in doubt
Is once to be resolv'd: exchange me for a goat,
When I shall turn the business of my soul
To such exsufflicate and blown surmises,
Matching thy inference. 'Tis not to make me jealous
To say my wife is fair, feeds well, loves company,
Is free of speech, sings, plays, and dances well;
Where virtue is, these are more virtuous:
Nor from mine own weak merits will I draw
The smallest fear or doubt of her revolt;
For she had eyes, and chose me. No, Iago;
I'll see before I doubt; when I doubt, prove;
And, on the proof, there is no more but this, —
Away at once with love or jealousy!

IAGO

I am glad of it; for now I shall have reason
To show the love and duty that I bear you
With franker spirit: therefore, as I am bound,
Receive it from me: — I speak not yet of proof.
Look to your wife; observe her well with Cassio;
Wear your eye thus, not jealous nor secure:
I would not have your free and noble nature,
Out of self-bounty, be abus'd; look to't:
I know our country disposition well;
In Venice they do let heaven see the pranks
They dare not show their husbands; their best
  conscience
Is — not to leave undone, but keep unknown.

OTHELLO

Dost thou say so?

IAGO

She did deceive her father, marrying you;
And when she seem'd to shake and fear your looks,

She lov'd them most.

OTHELLO

And so she did.

IAGO

Why, go to, then;
She that, so young, could give out such a seeming,
To seel her father's eyes up close as oak —
He thought 'twas witchcraft: — but I am much to blame;
I humbly do beseech you of your pardon
For too much loving you.

OTHELLO

I am bound to thee for ever.

IAGO

I see this hath a little dash'd your spirits.

OTHELLO

Not a jot, not a jot.

IAGO

I'faith, I fear it has.
I hope you will consider what is spoke
Comes from my love; — but I do see y'are moved: —
I am to pray you not to strain my speech
To grosser issues nor to larger reach
Than to suspicion.

OTHELLO

I will not.

IAGO

Should you do so, my lord,
My speech should fall into such vile success
As my thoughts aim not at. Cassio's my worthy friend: —
My lord, I see y' are mov'd.

OTHELLO

No, not much mov'd: —
I do not think but Desdemona's honest.

IAGO

Long live she so! and long live you to think so!

OTHELLO

And yet, how nature erring from itself, —

IAGO

Ay, there's the point: — as — to be bold with you —
Not to affect many proposed matches
Of her own clime, complexion, and degree,
Whereto we see in all things nature tends, —
Foh! one may smell in such, a will most rank,
Foul disproportion thoughts unnatural: —
But pardon me: I do not in position
Distinctly speak of her; though I may fear
Her will, recoiling to her better judgement,
May fall to match you with her country forms,
And happily repent.

OTHELLO

             Farewell, farewell:
If more thou dost perceive, let me know more;
Set on thy wife to observe: leave me, Iago.

IAGO

My lord, I take my leave.   *[Going.*

OTHELLO

Why did I marry? — This honest creature doubtless
Sees and knows more, much more, than he unfolds.

IAGO

My lord, I would I might entreat your honour   *[Returning.*
To scan this thing no further; leave it to time:
Although 'tis fit that Cassio have his place, —
For, sure, he fills it up with great ability, —
Yet, if you please to hold him off awhile,
You shall by that perceive him and his means:
Note if your lady strain his entertainment
With any strong or vehement importunity;
Much will be seen in that. In the mean time
Let me be thought too busy in my fears, —
As worthy cause I have to fear I am, —
And hold her free, I do beseech your honour.

OTHELLO
Fear not my government.

IAGO
I once more take my leave.   [*Exit.*

OTHELLO
This fellow's of exceeding honesty,
And knows all qualities, with a learned spirit,
Of human dealings. If I do prove her haggard,
Though that her jesses were my dear heartstrings,
I'ld whistle her off, and let her down the wind,
To prey at fortune. Haply, for I am black,
And have not those soft parts of conversation
That chamberers have; or, for I am declined
Into the vale of years, — yet that's not much; —
She's gone; I am abus'd; and my relief
Must be to loathe her. O curse of marriage,
That we can call these delicate creatures ours,
And not their appetites! I had rather be a toad,
And live upon the vapour of a dungeon,
Than keep a corner in the thing I love
For others' uses. Yet, 'tis the plague of great ones;
Prerogativ'd are they less than the base;
'Tis destiny unshunnable, like death:
Even then this forked plague is fated to us
When we do quicken. — Desdemona comes:
If she be false, O, then heaven mocks itself! —
I'll not believe't.

Enter DESDEMONA *and* EMILIA.

DESDEMONA
                    How now, my dear Othello!
Your dinner, and the generous islanders
By you invited, do attend your presence.

OTHELLO
I am to blame.

DESDEMONA
                    Why do you speak so faintly?
Are you not well?

OTHELLO
I have a pain upon my forehead here.

DESDEMONA
Faith, that's with watching; 'twill away again:
Let me but bind it hard, within this hour
It will be well.

OTHELLO
        Your napkin is too little;
      [*He puts the handkerchief from him; and she drops it.*
Let it alone. Come, I'll go in with you.

DESDEMONA
I am very sorry that you are not well.
           [*Exeunt* OTHELLO *and* DESDEMONA.

EMILIA
I am glad I have found this napkin:
This was her first remembrance from the Moor:
My wayward husband hath a hundred times
Woo'd me to steal it; but she so loves the token, —
For he conjured her she should ever keep it, —
That she reserves it evermore about her
To kiss and talk to. I'll have the work ta'en out,
And give't Iago:
What he will do with it heaven knows, not I;
I nothing but to please his fantasy.

        Enter IAGO.

IAGO
How now! what do you here alone?

EMILIA
Do not you chide; I have a thing for you.

IAGO
A thing for me! — it is a common thing —

EMILIA
Ha!

IAGO
To have a foolish wife.

EMILIA

O, is that all? What will you give me now
For that same handkerchief?

IAGO

What handkerchief?

EMILIA

What handkerchief!
Why, that the Moor first gave to Desdemona;
That which so often you did bid me steal.

IAGO

Hast stol'n it from her?

EMILIA

No, faith; she let it drop by negligence,
And, to th'advantage, I, being here, took't up.
Look, here it is.

IAGO

A good wench; give it me.

EMILIA

What will you do with't, that you have been so earnest
To have me filch it?

IAGO

Why, what's that to you?   [*Snatching it.*

EMILIA

If't be not for some purpose of import,
Give't me again: poor lady, she'll run mad
When she shall lack it.

IAGO

Be not acknown on't; I have use for it.
Go, leave me.   [*Exit* EMILIA.
I will in Cassio's lodging lose this napkin,
And let him find it. Trifles light as air
Are to the jealous confirmations strong
As proofs of holy writ: this may do something.
The Moor already changes with my poison: —
Dangerous conceits are, in their natures, poisons,
Which at the first are scarce found to distaste,
But, with a little, act upon the blood,

73

Burn like the mines of sulphur. — I did say so: —
Look, where he comes! Not poppy, nor mandragora,
Nor all the drowsy syrups of the world,
Shall ever medicine thee to that sweet sleep
Which thou owedst yesterday.

Enter OTHELLO.

OTHELLO

                    Ha! ha! false to me?

IAGO

Why, how now, general! no more of that.

OTHELLO

Avaunt! be gone! thou hast set me on the rack: —
I swear 'tis better to be much abused
Than but to know't a little.

IAGO

               How now, my lord!

OTHELLO

What sense had I of her stol'n hours of lust?
I saw't not, thought it not, it harm'd not me:
I slept the next night well, was free and merry;
I found not Cassio's kisses on her lips:
He that is robb'd, not wanting what is stol'n,
Let him not know't, and he's not robb'd at all.

IAGO

I am sorry to hear this.

OTHELLO

I had been happy, if the general camp,
Pioners and all, had tasted her sweet body,
So I had nothing known. O, now, for ever
Farewell the tranquil mind! farewell content!
Farewell the plumed troop, and the big wars,
That make ambition virtue! O, farewell!
Farewell the neighing steed, and the shrill trump,
The spirit-stirring drum, th'ear-piercing fife,
The royal banner, and all quality,
Pride, pomp and circumstance of glorious war!
And, O you mortal engines, whose rude throats

Th'immortal Jove's dread clamours counterfeit,
Farewell! Othello's occupation's gone!

IAGO

Is't possible, my lord?

OTHELLO

Villain, be sure thou prove my love a whore, —
Be sure of it; give me the ocular proof;
Or, by the worth of man's eternal soul,
Thou hadst been better have been born a dog
Than answer my wak'd wrath!

IAGO

                    Is't come to this?

OTHELLO

Make me to see't; or, at the least, so prove it,
That the probation bear no hinge nor loop
To hang a doubt on; or woe upon thy life!

IAGO

My noble lord, —

OTHELLO

If thou dost slander her, and torture me,
Never pray more; abandon all remorse;
On horror's head horrors accumulate;
Do deeds to make heaven weep, all earth amazed;
For nothing canst thou to damnation add
Greater than that.

IAGO

           O grace! O heaven forgive me!
Are you a man? have you a soul or sense? —
God be wi'you! take mine office. — O wretched fool,
That livest to make thine honesty a vice! —
O monstrous world! Take note, take note, O world,
To be direct and honest is not safe. —
I thank you for this profit; and from hence
I'll love no friend, sith love breeds such offence.

OTHELLO

Nay, stay: — thou shouldst be honest.

IAGO

  I should be wise; for honesty's a fool,
  And loses that it works for.

OTHELLO

               By the world,
  I think my wife be honest, and think she is not;
  I think that thou art just, and think thou art not;
  I'll have some proof: her name, that was as fresh
  As Dian's visage, is now begrim'd and black
  As mine own face. — If there be cords or knives,
  Poison, or fire, or suffocating streams,
  I'll not endure it. — Would I were satisfied!

IAGO

  I see, sir, you are eaten up with passion:
  I do repent me that I put it to you.
  You would be satisfied?

OTHELLO

               Would! nay, I will.

IAGO

  And may: but, how? how satisfied, my lord?
  Would you, the supervisor, grossly gape on, —
  Behold her topp'd?

OTHELLO

             Death and damnation! O!

IAGO

  It were a tedious difficulty, I think,
  To bring them to that prospect: damn them, then,
  If ever mortal eyes do see them bolster
  More than their own! What then? how then?
  What shall I say? Where's satisfaction?
  It is impossible you should see this,
  Were they as prime as goats, as hot as monkeys,
  As salt as wolves in pride, and fools as gross
  As ignorance made drunk. But yet, I say,
  If imputation and strong circumstances —
  Which lead directly to the door of truth —
  Will give you satisfaction, you may have't.

OTHELLO

Give me a living reason she's disloyal.

IAGO

I do not like the office:
But, sith I am enter'd in this cause so far, —
Prick'd to't by foolish honesty and love, —
I will go on. I lay with Cassio lately;
And, being troubled with a raging tooth,
I could not sleep.
There are a kind of men so loose of soul
That in their sleeps will mutter their affairs;
One of this kind is Cassio:
In sleep I heard him say, 'Sweet Desdemona,
Let us be wary, let us hide our loves';
And then, sir, would he gripe and wring my hand,
Cry 'O sweet creature!' and then kiss me hard,
As if he pluck'd up kisses by the roots
That grew upon my lips: then laid his leg
Over my thigh, and sigh'd, and kiss'd; and then
Cried, 'Cursed fate that gave thee to the Moor!'

OTHELLO

O monstrous! monstrous!

IAGO

                Nay, this was but his dream.

OTHELLO

But this denoted a foregone conclusion:
'Tis a shrewd doubt, though it be but a dream.

IAGO

And this may help to thicken other proofs
That do demonstrate thinly.

OTHELLO

              I'll tear her all to pieces.

IAGO

Nay, but be wise: yet we see nothing done;
She may be honest yet. Tell me but this, —
Have you not sometimes seen a handkerchief
Spotted with strawberries in your wife's hand?

OTHELLO

I gave her such a one; 'twas my first gift.

IAGO

I know not that: but such a handkerchief —
I am sure it was your wife's — did I to-day
See Cassio wipe his beard with.

OTHELLO

If it be that, —

IAGO

If it be that, or any that was hers,
It speaks against her with the other proofs.

OTHELLO

O, that the slave had forty thousand lives, —
One is too poor, too weak for my revenge!
Now do I see 'tis true. — Look here, Iago;
All my fond love thus do I blow to heaven:
'Tis gone. —
Arise, black vengeance, from thy hollow hell!
Yield up, O love, thy crown and hearted throne
To tyrannous hate! Swell, bosom, with thy fraught,
For 'tis of aspics' tongues!

IAGO

Yet be content.

OTHELLO

O, blood, blood, blood!

IAGO

Patience, I say; your mind perhaps may change.

OTHELLO

Never, Iago. Like to the Pontic sea,
Whose icy current and compulsive course
Ne'er feels retiring ebb, but keeps due on
To the Propontic and the Hellespont;
Even so my bloody thoughts, with violent pace,
Shall ne'er look back, ne'er ebb to humble love,
Till that a capable and wide revenge
Swallow them up. — Now, by yond marble heaven,
In the due reverence of a sacred vow   [*Kneels.*

I here engage my words.

IAGO

                   Do not rise yet. —   [*Kneels.*

Witness, you ever-burning lights above,

You elements that clip us round about, —

OTHELLO Now, by yond marble heaven, in the due reverence of a sacred
       vow I here engage my words.

Witness that here Iago doth give up
The execution of his wit, hands, heart,
To wrong'd Othello's service! Let him command,
And to obey shall be in me remorse,
What bloody business ever.   *[They rise.*

OTHELLO

                I greet thy love,
Not with vain thanks, but with acceptance bounteous,
And will upon the instant put thee to't:
Within these three days let me hear thee say
That Cassio's not alive.

IAGO

My friend is dead; 'tis done at your request:
But let her live.

OTHELLO

          Damn her, lewd minx! O, damn her!
Come, go with me apart; I will withdraw,
To furnish me with some swift means of death
For the fair devil. Now art thou my lieutenant.

IAGO

I am your own for ever.   *[Exeunt.*

SCENE IV

Before the castle.

Enter DESDEMONA, EMILIA, *and* CLOWN.

DESDEMONA

Do you know, sirrah, where Lieutenant Cassio lies?

CLOWN

I dare not say he lies any where.

DESDEMONA

Why, man?

CLOWN

He's a soldier; and for one to say a soldier lies, is stabbing.

DESDEMONA

Go to: where lodges he?

CLOWN

To tell you where he lodges, is to tell you where I lie.

DESDEMONA

Can any thing be made of this?

CLOWN

I know not where he lodges; and for me to devise a
lodging, and say he lies here or he lies there, were to lie
in mine own throat.

DESDEMONA

Can you inquire him out, and be edified by report?

CLOWN

I will catechise the world for him; that is, make
questions, and by them answer.

DESDEMONA

Seek him, bid him come hither: tell him I have moved
my lord on his behalf, and hope all will be well.

CLOWN

To do this is within the compass of man's wit; and
therefore I will attempt the doing it.   [*Exit.*

DESDEMONA

Where should I lose that handkerchief, Emilia?

EMILIA

I know not, madam.

DESDEMONA

Believe me, I had rather have lost my purse
Full of crusadoes: and, but my noble Moor
Is true of mind, and made of no such baseness
As jealous creatures are, it were enough
To put him to ill thinking.

EMILIA

                    Is he not jealous?

DESDEMONA

Who, he? I think the sun where he was born
Drew all such humours from him.

EMILIA

                    Look, where he comes.

DESDEMONA

I will not leave him now till Cassio
Be call'd to him.

Enter OTHELLO.
How is't with you, my lord?

OTHELLO

Well, my good lady. — [*aside*] O, hardness to dissemble! —
How do you, Desdemona?

DESDEMONA

Well, my good lord.

OTHELLO

Give me your hand: this hand is moist, my lady.

DESDEMONA

It yet hath felt no age nor known no sorrow.

OTHELLO

This argues fruitfulness and liberal heart: —
Hot, hot, and moist: this hand of yours requires
A sequester from liberty, fasting and prayer,
Much castigation, exercise devout;
For here's a young and sweating devil here,
That commonly rebels. 'Tis a good hand,
A frank one.

DESDEMONA

You may, indeed, say so;
For 'twas that hand that gave away my heart.

OTHELLO

A liberal hand: the hearts of old gave hands;
But our new heraldry is hands, not hearts.

DESDEMONA

I cannot speak of this. Come now, your promise.

OTHELLO

What promise, chuck?

DESDEMONA

I have sent to bid Cassio come speak with you.

OTHELLO

I have a salt and sorry rheum offends me;

Lend me thy handkerchief.

DESDEMONA

Here, my lord.

OTHELLO

That which I gave you.

DESDEMONA

I have it not about me.

OTHELLO

Not?

DESDEMONA

No, indeed, my lord.

OTHELLO

That is a fault.

That handkerchief
Did an Egyptian to my mother give;
She was a charmer, and could almost read
The thoughts of people: she told her, while she kept it,
'Twould make her amiable, and subdue my father
Entirely to her love; but if she lost it,
Or made gift of it, my father's eye
Should hold her loathed, and his spirits should hunt
After new fancies: she, dying, gave it me;
And bid me, when my fate would have me wive,
To give it her. I did so: and take heed on't;
Make it a darling like your precious eye;
To lose't or give't away were such perdition
As nothing else could match.

DESDEMONA

Is't possible?

OTHELLO

'Tis true: there's magic in the web of it:
A sibyl, that had number'd in the world
The sun to course two hundred compasses,
In her prophetic fury sew'd the work;
The worms were hallow'd that did breed the silk;
And it was dyed in mummy which the skilful
Conserv'd of maidens' hearts.

DESDEMONA

Indeed! is't true?

OTHELLO

Most veritable; therefore look to't well.

DESDEMONA

Then would to God that I had never seen't!

OTHELLO

Ha! wherefore?

DESDEMONA

Why do you speak so startingly and rash?

OTHELLO

Is't lost? Is't gone? speak; is't out o'the way?

DESDEMONA

Heaven bless us!

OTHELLO

Say you?

DESDEMONA

It is not lost; but what an if it were?

OTHELLO

How!

DESDEMONA

I say, it is not lost.

OTHELLO

Fetch't, let me see't.

DESDEMONA

Why, so I can, sir, but I will not now.
This is a trick to put me from my suit:
Pray you, let Cassio be receiv'd again.

OTHELLO

Fetch me the handkerchief: my mind misgives.

DESDEMONA

Come, come;
You'll never meet a more sufficient man.

OTHELLO

The handkerchief!

DESDEMONA

          I pray, talk me of Cassio.

OTHELLO

The handkerchief!

DESDEMONA

          A man that all his time
Hath founded his good fortunes on your love,
Shared dangers with you, —

OTHELLO

The handkerchief!

DESDEMONA

In sooth, you are to blame.

OTHELLO

Away!   [*Exit.*

EMILIA

Is not this man jealous?

DESDEMONA

I ne'er saw this before.
Sure, there's some wonder in this handkerchief:
I am most unhappy in the loss of it.

EMILIA

'Tis not a year or two shows us a man:
They are all but stomachs, and we all but food;
They eat us hungerly, and when they are full,
They belch us. — Look you, — Cassio and my
   husband.

          Enter CASSIO *and* IAGO.

IAGO

There is no other way; 'tis she must do't:
And, lo, the happiness! go, and importune her.

DESDEMONA

How now, good Cassio! what's the news with you?

CASSIO

Madam, my former suit: I do beseech you
That by your virtuous means I may again
Exist, and be a member of his love

Whom I with all the office of my heart
Entirely honour: I would not be delay'd.
If my offence be of such mortal kind
That nor my service past, nor present sorrows,
Nor purpos'd merit in futurity,
Can ransom me into his love again,
But to know so must be my benefit;
So shall I clothe me in a forc'd content,
And shut myself up in some other course,
To fortune's alms.

DESDEMONA

                 Alas, thrice-gentle Cassio!
My advocation is not now in tune;
My lord is not my lord; nor should I know him,
Were he in favour as in humour alter'd.
So help me every spirit sanctified,
As I have spoken for you all my best,
And stood within the blank of his displeasure
For my free speech! you must awhile be patient:
What I can do I will; and more I will
Than for myself I dare: let that suffice you.

IAGO

Is my lord angry?

EMILIA

               He went hence but now,
And certainly in strange unquietness.

IAGO

Can he be angry? I have seen the cannon,
When it hath blown his ranks into the air,
And, like the devil, from his very arm
Puff'd his own brother; — and can he be angry?
Something of moment, then: I will go meet him:
There's matter in't indeed, if he be angry.

DESDEMONA

I prithee, do so.   [*Exit* IAGO.
         Something, sure, of state, —
Either from Venice, or some unhatch'd practice

Made demonstrable here in Cyprus to him, —
Hath puddled his clear spirit; and in such cases
Men's natures wrangle with inferior things,
Though great ones are their object. 'Tis even so;
For let our finger ache, and it indues
Our other healthful members even to that sense
Of pain: nay, we must think men are not gods,
Nor of them look for such observancy
As fits the bridal. — Beshrew me much, Emilia,
I was — unhandsome warrior as I am —
Arraigning his unkindness with my soul;
But now I find I had suborn'd the witness,
And he's indicted falsely.

EMILIA

Pray heaven it be state-matters, as you think,
And no conception nor no jealous toy
Concerning you.

DESDEMONA

Alas the day, I never gave him cause!

EMILIA

But jealous souls will not be answer'd so;
They are not ever jealous for the cause,
But jealous for they're jealous: it is a monster
Begot upon itself, born on itself.

DESDEMONA

Heaven keep that monster from Othello's mind!

EMILIA

Lady, amen.

DESDEMONA

I will go seek him. — Cassio, walk hereabout:
If I do find him fit, I'll move your suit,
And seek to effect it to my uttermost.

CASSIO

I humbly thank your ladyship.

> [*Exeunt* DESDEMONA *and* EMILIA.
> *Enter* BIANCA.

BIANCA

Save you, friend Cassio!

CASSIO

                    What make you from home?
How is it with you, my most fair Bianca?
I'faith, sweet love, I was coming to your house.

BIANCA

And I was going to your lodging, Cassio.
What, keep a week away? seven days and nights?
Eight score eight hours? and lovers' absent hours
More tedious than the dial eight score times?
O weary reckoning!

CASSIO

                    Pardon me, Bianca:
I have this while with leaden thoughts been press'd;
But I shall, in a more continuate time,
Strike off this score of absence. Sweet Bianca,
            [*Giving her* DESDEMONA'S *handkerchief.*
Take me this work out.

BIANCA

                    O Cassio, whence came this?
This is some token from a newer friend:
To the felt absence now I feel a cause:
Is't come to this? Well, well.

CASSIO

                    Go to, woman!
Throw your vile guesses in the devil's teeth,
From whence you have them. You are jealous now
That this is from some mistress, some remembrance:
No, in good troth, Bianca.

BIANCA

                    Why, whose is it?

CASSIO

I know not neither: I found it in my chamber.
I like the work well: ere it be demanded, —
As like enough it will, — I'd have it copied:
Take it, and do't; and leave me for this time.

BIANCA
Leave you! wherefore?

CASSIO
I do attend here on the general;
And think it no addition, nor my wish,
To have him see me woman'd.

BIANCA
                    Why, I pray you?

CASSIO
Not that I love you not.

BIANCA
                But that you do not love me.
I pray you, bring me on the way a little;
And say if I shall see you soon at night.

CASSIO
'Tis but a little way that I can bring you;
For I attend here: but I'll see you soon.

BIANCA
'Tis very good; I must be circumstanc'd.   *[Exeunt.*

ACT IV

SCENE I

Cyprus. Before the castle.
Enter OTHELLO *and* IAGO.

IAGO
Will you think so?

OTHELLO
            Think so, Iago!

IAGO
                    What,
To kiss in private?

OTHELLO
                An unauthoris'd kiss.

IAGO

  Or to be naked with her friend in bed
  An hour or more, not meaning any harm?

OTHELLO

  Naked in bed, Iago, and not mean harm!
  It is hypocrisy against the devil:
  They that mean virtuously and yet do so,
  The devil their virtue tempts, and they tempt heaven.

IAGO

  So they do nothing, 'tis a venial slip:
  But if I give my wife a handkerchief, —

OTHELLO

  What then?

IAGO

  Why, then, 'tis hers, my lord; and, being hers,
  She may, I think, bestow't on any man.

OTHELLO

  She is protectress of her honour too:
  May she give that?

IAGO

  Her honour is an essence that's not seen;
  They have it very oft that have it not:
  But, for the handkerchief, —

OTHELLO

  By heaven, I would most gladly have forgot it: —
  Thou said'st, — O, it comes o'er my memory,
  As doth the raven o'er the infected house,
  Boding to all, — he had my handkerchief.

IAGO

  Ay, what of that?

OTHELLO

            That's not so good now.

IAGO

                        What,
  If I had said I had seen him do you wrong?
  Or heard him say, — as knaves be such abroad,
  Who having, by their own importunate suit,

Or voluntary dotage of some mistress,
Convinced or supplied them, cannot choose
But they must blab —

OTHELLO

                Hath he said any thing?

IAGO

He hath, my lord; but be you well assured,
No more than he'll unswear.

OTHELLO

                  What hath he said?

IAGO

Faith, that he did — I know not what he did.

OTHELLO

What? what?

IAGO

Lie —

OTHELLO

    With her?

IAGO

            With her, on her; what you will.

OTHELLO

Lie with her! lie on her! — We say lie on her, when they
belie her. — Lie with her! that's fulsome. —
Handkerchief — confessions — handkerchief! — To
confess, and be hang'd for his labour; — first, to be
hang'd, and then to confess. — I tremble at it. Nature
would not invest herself in such shadowing passion
without some instruction. It is not words that shake me
thus: — pish! — noses, ears, and lips. — Is't possible?
— Confess — handkerchief! — O devil! —

                      [*Falls in a trance.*

IAGO

Work on,
My medicine, work! Thus credulous fools are caught;
And many worthy and chaste dames even thus,
All guiltless, meet reproach. — What, ho! my lord!
My lord, I say! Othello!

Enter CASSIO.
How now, Cassio!

CASSIO
  What's the matter?

IAGO
  My lord is fall'n into an epilepsy:

IAGO Work on, my medicine, work!

This is his second fit; he had one yesterday.

CASSIO

Rub him about the temples.

IAGO

             No, forbear;
The lethargy must have his quiet course:
If not, he foams at mouth, and by and by
Breaks out to savage madness. Look, he stirs:
Do you withdraw yourself a little while,
He will recover straight: when he is gone,
I would on great occasion speak with you.

                     [*Exit* CASSIO.

How is it, general? have you not hurt your head?

OTHELLO

Dost thou mock me?

IAGO

             I mock you! no, by heaven.
Would you would bear your fortune like a man!

OTHELLO

A horned man's a monster and a beast.

IAGO

There's many a beast, then, in a populous city,
And many a civil monster.

OTHELLO

Did he confess it?

IAGO

             Good sir, be a man;
Think every bearded fellow that's but yok'd
May draw with you: there's millions now alive
That nightly lie in those unproper beds
Which they dare swear peculiar: your case is better.
O, 'tis the spite of hell, the fiend's arch-mock,
To lip a wanton in a secure couch,
And to suppose her chaste! No, let me know;
And knowing what I am, I know what she shall be.

OTHELLO

O, thou art wise; 'tis certain.

IAGO
                                   Stand you awhile apart;
Confine yourself but in a patient list.
Whilst you were here o'erwhelmed with your grief, —
A passion most unfitting such a man, —
Cassio came hither: I shifted him away,
And laid good'scuse upon your ecstasy;
Bade him anon return, and here speak with me;
The which he promis'd. Do but encave yourself,
And mark the fleers, the gibes, and notable scorns,
That dwell in every region of his face;
For I will make him tell the tale anew, —
Where, how, how oft, how long ago, and when
He hath, and is again to cope your wife:
I say, but mark his gesture. Marry, patience;
Or I shall say y'are all in all in spleen,
And nothing of a man.

OTHELLO
                              Dost thou hear, Iago?
I will be found most cunning in my patience;
But — dost thou hear? — most bloody.

IAGO
                                   That's not amiss;
But yet keep time in all. Will you withdraw?
                                   [OTHELLO *retires.*
Now will I question Cassio of Bianca,
A housewife that, by selling her desires,
Buys herself bread and clothes: it is a creature
That dotes on Cassio, — as 'tis the strumpet's plague
To beguile many and be beguil'd by one: —
He, when he hears of her, cannot refrain
From the excess of laughter: — here he comes: —
As he shall smile, Othello shall go mad;
And his unbookish jealousy must construe
Poor Cassio's smiles, gestures, and light behaviour,
Quite in the wrong.

                    Enter CASSIO.
                    How do you now, lieutenant?

CASSIO

The worser that you give me the addition
Whose want even kills me.

IAGO

Ply Desdemona well, and you are sure on't.
Now, if this suit lay in Bianca's power,   [*Speaking lower.*
How quickly should you speed!

CASSIO

                       Alas, poor caitiff!

OTHELLO [*aside*].

Look, how he laughs already!

IAGO

I never knew woman love man so.

CASSIO

Alas, poor rogue! I think, i'faith, she loves me.

OTHELLO [*aside*].

Now he denies it faintly, and laughs it out.

IAGO

Do you hear, Cassio?

OTHELLO [*aside*].

                  Now he importunes him
To tell it o'er: — go to; well said, well said.

IAGO

She gives it out that you shall marry her:
Do you intend it?

CASSIO

Ha, ha, ha!

OTHELLO [*aside*].

Do you triumph, Roman? do you triumph?

CASSIO

I marry her! — what, a customer! Prithee, bear some
charity to my wit; do not think it so unwholesome: —
ha, ha, ha!

OTHELLO [*aside*].

So, so, so, so: — they laugh that win.

IAGO

Faith, the cry goes that you shall marry her.

CASSIO

Prithee, say true.

IAGO

I am a very villain else.

OTHELLO [*aside*].

Have you scored me? Well.

CASSIO

This is the monkey's own giving out: she is persuaded I will marry her, out of her own love and flattery, not out of my promise.

OTHELLO [*aside*].

Iago beckons me; now he begins the story.

CASSIO

She was here even now; she haunts me in every place. I was, the other day, talking on the sea-bank with certain Venetians; and thither comes the bauble, and by this hand she falls me thus about my neck, —

OTHELLO [*aside*].

Crying 'O dear Cassio!' as it were: his gesture imports it.

CASSIO

So hangs, and lolls, and weeps upon me; so hales and pulls me: — ha, ha, ha!

OTHELLO [*aside*].

Now he tells how she pluck'd him to my chamber. O, I see that nose of yours, but not that dog I shall throw it to.

CASSIO

Well, I must leave her company.

IAGO

Before me! look, where she comes.

CASSIO

'Tis such another fitchew! marry, a perfum'd one.

Enter BIANCA.

What do you mean by this haunting of me?

BIANCA

Let the devil and his dam haunt you! What did you
mean by that same handkerchief you gave me even now?
I was a fine fool to take it. I must take out the work? —
A likely piece of work, that you should find it in your
chamber, and not know who left it there! This is some
minx's token, and I must take out the work? There, —
give it your hobby-horse: wheresoever you had it, I'll
take out no work on't.

CASSIO

How now, my sweet Bianca! how now! how now!

OTHELLO [*aside*].

By heaven, that should be my handkerchief!

BIANCA

An you'll come to supper to-night, you may; an you will
not, come when you are next prepared for.   [*Exit.*

IAGO

After her, after her.

CASSIO

Faith, I must; she'll rail i' the street else.

IAGO

Will you sup there?

CASSIO

Faith, I intend so.

IAGO

Well, I may chance to see you; for I would very fain
speak with you.

CASSIO

Prithee, come; will you?

IAGO

Go to; say no more.   [*Exit* CASSIO.

OTHELLO [*coming forward*].

How shall I murder him; Iago?

IAGO

Did you perceive how he laugh'd at his vice?

OTHELLO

O Iago!

IAGO

And did you see the handkerchief?

OTHELLO

Was that mine?

IAGO

Yours, by this hand: and to see how he prizes the foolish woman your wife! she gave it him, and he hath given it his whore.

OTHELLO

I would have him nine years a-killing. — A fine woman! a fair woman! a sweet woman!

IAGO

Nay, you must forget that.

OTHELLO

Ay, let her rot, and perish, and be damn'd to-night; for she shall not live: no, my heart is turn'd to stone; I strike it, and it hurts my hand. — O, the world hath not a sweeter creature: she might lie by an emperor's side, and command him tasks.

IAGO

Nay, that's not your way.

OTHELLO

Hang her! I do but say what she is: — so delicate with her needle! — an admirable musician! O, she will sing the savageness out of a bear! — of so high and plenteous wit and invention! —

IAGO

She's the worse for all this.

OTHELLO

O, a thousand thousand times: — and then, of so gentle a condition!

IAGO

Ay, too gentle.

OTHELLO

Nay, that's certain: — but yet the pity of it, Iago!
O Iago, the pity of it, Iago!

IAGO

If you are so fond over her iniquity, give her patent to
offend; for, if it touch not you, it comes near nobody.

OTHELLO

I will chop her into messes: — cuckold me!

IAGO

O, 'tis foul in her.

OTHELLO

With mine officer!

IAGO

That's fouler.

OTHELLO

Get me some poison, Iago; this night: — I'll not
expostulate with her, lest her body and beauty
unprovide my mind again: — this night, Iago.

IAGO

Do it not with poison, strangle her in her bed, even the
bed she hath contaminated.

OTHELLO

Good, good: the justice of it pleases: very good.

IAGO

And for Cassio, — let me be his undertaker: you shall
hear more by midnight.

OTHELLO

Excellent good. [*A trumpet within.*] What trumpet is that
same?

IAGO

Something from Venice, sure. 'Tis Lodovico
Come from the duke: and, see, your wife is with him.

Enter LODOVICO, DESDEMONA, *and*
ATTENDANTS.

LODOVICO

Save you, worthy general!

OTHELLO

With all my heart, sir.

LODOVICO

The duke and senators of Venice greet you.

[*Gives him a packet.*

OTHELLO

I kiss the instrument of their pleasures.

[*Opens the packet, and reads.*

DESDEMONA

And what's the news, good cousin Lodovico?

IAGO

I am very glad to see you, signior;
Welcome to Cyprus.

LODOVICO

I thank you. How does Lieutenant Cassio?

IAGO

Lives, sir.

DESDEMONA

Cousin, there's fall'n between him and my lord
An unkind breach: but you shall make all well.

OTHELLO

Are you sure of that?

DESDEMONA

My lord?

OTHELLO [*reads*].

This fail you not to do, as you will —

LODOVICO

He did not call; he's busy in the paper.
Is there division 'twixt my lord and Cassio?

DESDEMONA

A most unhappy one: I would do much
T'atone them, for the love I bear to Cassio.

OTHELLO

Fire and brimstone!

DESDEMONA

My lord?

OTHELLO

Are you wise?

DESDEMONA

What, is he angry?

LODOVICO

May be the letter mov'd him;
For, as I think, they do command him home,
Deputing Cassio in his government.

DESDEMONA

Trust me, I am glad on't.

OTHELLO

Indeed!

DESDEMONA

My lord?

OTHELLO

I am glad to see you mad.

DESDEMONA

Why, sweet Othello, —

OTHELLO

Devil! [*Striking her.*

DESDEMONA

I have not deserv'd this.

LODOVICO

My lord, this would not be believed in Venice,
Though I should swear I saw't: 'tis very much:
Make her amends; she weeps.

OTHELLO

O devil, devil!
If that the earth could teem with woman's tears,
Each drop she falls would prove a crocodile. —
Out of my sight!

DESDEMONA

I will not stay to offend you. [*Going.*

LODOVICO

Truly, an obedient lady: —
I do beseech your lordship, call her back.

OTHELLO
Mistress!

DESDEMONA
      My lord?

OTHELLO
            What would you with her, sir?

LODOVICO
Who, I, my lord?

OTHELLO
Ay; you did wish that I would make her turn:
Sir, she can turn, and turn, and yet go on,
And turn again; and she can weep, sir, weep;
And she's obedient, as you say, — obedient, —
Very obedient. — Proceed you in your tears. —
Concerning this, sir, — O well-painted passion! —
I am commanded home. — Get you away;
I'll send for you anon. — Sir, I obey the mandate,
And will return to Venice. — Hence, avaunt!
                  [*Exit* DESDEMONA.
Cassio shall have my place. And, sir, to-night
I do entreat that we may sup together:
You are welcome, sir, to Cyprus. — Goats and monkeys!
                       [*Exit.*

LODOVICO
Is this the noble Moor whom our full senate
Call all-in-all sufficient? — Is this the nature
Whom passion could not shake? whose solid virtue
The shot of accident, nor dart of chance,
Could neither graze nor pierce?

IAGO
                  He is much changed.

LODOVICO
Are his wits safe? is he not light of brain?

IAGO
He's that he is: I may not breathe my censure.
What he might be, — if, what he might, he is not, —
I would to heaven he were!

LODOVICO

What, strike his wife!

IAGO

Faith, that was not so well; yet would I knew
That stroke would prove the worst!

LODOVICO

Is it his use?
Or did the letters work upon his blood,
And new-create this fault?

IAGO

Alas, alas!
It is not honesty in me to speak
What I have seen and known. You shall observe him;
And his own courses will denote him so,
That I may save my speech: do but go after,
And mark how he continues.

LODOVICO

I am sorry that I am deceiv'd in him.   [*Exeunt.*

SCENE II

A room in the castle.

Enter OTHELLO *and* EMILIA.

OTHELLO

You have seen nothing, then?

EMILIA

Nor ever heard, nor ever did suspect.

OTHELLO

Yes, you have seen Cassio and she together.

EMILIA

But then I saw no harm, and then I heard
Each syllable that breath made up between them.

OTHELLO

What, did they never whisper?

EMILIA

Never, my lord.

OTHELLO
Nor send you out o'th'way?

EMILIA
Never.

OTHELLO
To fetch her fan, her gloves, her mask, nor nothing?

EMILIA
Never, my lord.

OTHELLO
That's strange.

EMILIA
I durst, my lord, to wager she is honest,
Lay down my soul at stake: if you think other,
Remove your thought, — it doth abuse your bosom.
If any wretch have put this in your head,
Let heaven requite it with the serpent's curse!
For, if she be not honest, chaste, and true,
There's no man happy; the purest of their wives
Is foul as slander.

OTHELLO
        Bid her come hither: — go.
                [*Exit* EMILIA.
She says enough; — yet she's a simple bawd
That cannot say as much. This is a subtle whore,
A closet-lock-and-key of villainous secrets:
And yet she'll kneel and pray; I have seen her do't.

       Enter DESDEMONA *with* EMILIA.

DESDEMONA
My lord, what is your will?

OTHELLO
             Pray, chuck, come hither.

DESDEMONA
What is your pleasure?

OTHELLO
           Let me see your eyes;
Look in my face.

DESDEMONA
>   What horrible fancy's this?

OTHELLO [*to* EMILIA].
  Some of your function, mistress;
  Leave procreants alone, and shut the door;
  Cough, or cry 'hem', if anybody come:
  Your mystery, your mystery; — nay, dispatch.
>   [*Exit* EMILIA.

DESDEMONA
  Upon my knees, what doth your speech import?
  I understand a fury in your words,
  But not the words.

OTHELLO
  Why, what art thou?

DESDEMONA Upon my knees, what doth your speech import?

DESDEMONA

     Your wife, my lord; your true
And loyal wife.

OTHELLO

     Come, swear it, damn thyself;
Lest, being like one of heaven, the devils themselves
Should fear to seize thee: therefore be double damn'd, —
Swear thou art honest.

DESDEMONA

     Heaven doth truly know it.

OTHELLO

Heaven truly knows that thou art false as hell.

DESDEMONA

To whom, my lord? with whom? how am I false?

OTHELLO

Ah, Desdemona! — away! away! away!

DESDEMONA

Alas the heavy day! — Why do you weep?
Am I the motive of these tears, my lord?
If haply you my father do suspect
An instrument of this your calling back,
Lay not your blame on me: if you have lost him,
Why, I have lost him too.

OTHELLO

     Had it pleas'd heaven
To try me with affliction; had they rain'd
All kinds of sores and shames on my bare head;
Steep'd me in poverty to the very lips;
Given to captivity me and my utmost hopes;
I should have found in some place of my soul
A drop of patience: but, alas, to make me
A fixed figure for the time of scorn
To point his slow unmoving finger at! —
Yet could I bear that too; well, very well:
But there, where I have garner'd up my heart,
Where either I must live, or bear no life, —
The fountain from the which my current runs,

Or else dries up; to be discarded thence!
Or keep it as a cistern for foul toads
To knot and gender in! — turn thy complexion there,
Patience, thou young and rose-lipp'd cherubin, —
Ay, there, look grim as hell!

DESDEMONA

I hope my noble lord esteems me honest.

OTHELLO

O, ay; as summer flies are in the shambles,
That quicken even with blowing. O thou weed,
Who art so lovely fair, and smell'st so sweet,
That the sense aches at thee, — would thou hadst ne'er
  been born!

DESDEMONA

Alas, what ignorant sin have I committed?

OTHELLO

Was this fair paper, this most goodly book,
Made to write 'whore' upon? What committed!
Committed! — O thou public commoner!
I should make very forges of my cheeks,
That would to cinders burn up modesty,
Did I but speak thy deeds. — What committed!
Heaven stops the nose at it, and the moon winks;
The bawdy wind, that kisses all it meets,
Is hush'd within the hollow mine of earth,
And will not hear it. — What committed! —
Impudent strumpet!

DESDEMONA

                              By heaven, you do me wrong.

OTHELLO

Are you not a strumpet?

DESDEMONA

                              No, as I am a Christian:
If to preserve this vessel for my lord
From any other foul unlawful touch,
Be not to be a strumpet, I am none.

OTHELLO

What, not a whore?

DESDEMONA

     No, as I shall be saved.

OTHELLO

Is't possible?

DESDEMONA

O, heaven forgive us!

OTHELLO

    I cry you mercy, then:
I took you for that cunning whore of Venice
That married with Othello. — You, mistress,
That have the office opposite to Saint Peter,
And keep the gate of hell!

     Enter EMILIA.
     You, you, ay, you!
We have done our course; there's money for your pains:
I pray you, turn the key, and keep our counsel. [*Exit.*

EMILIA

Alas, what does this gentleman conceive? —
How do you, madam? how do you, my good lady?

DESDEMONA

Faith, half asleep.

EMILIA

Good madam, what's the matter with my lord?

DESDEMONA

With who?

EMILIA

Why, with my lord, madam.

DESDEMONA

Who is thy lord?

EMILIA

    He that is yours, sweet lady.

DESDEMONA

I have none: do not talk to me, Emilia;
I cannot weep; nor answer have I none,
But what should go by water. Prithee, to-night

Lay on my bed my wedding-sheets, — remember; —
And call thy husband hither.

EMILIA

>Here's a change indeed!

>>[*Exit.*

DESDEMONA

'Tis meet I should be us'd so, very meet.
How have I been behav'd, that he might stick
The small'st opinion on my least misuse?

Enter EMILIA *with* IAGO.

IAGO

What is your pleasure, madam? How is't with you?

DESDEMONA

I cannot tell. Those that do teach young babes
Do it with gentle means and easy tasks:
He might have chid me so; for, in good faith,
I am a child to chiding.

IAGO

>What's the matter, lady?

EMILIA

Alas, Iago, my lord hath so bewhored her,
Thrown such despite and heavy terms upon her,
As true hearts cannot bear.

DESDEMONA

Am I that name, Iago?

IAGO

>What name, fair lady?

DESDEMONA

Such as she says my lord did say I was.

EMILIA

He call'd her whore: a beggar in his drink
Could not have laid such terms upon his callet.

IAGO

Why did he so?

DESDEMONA

I do not know; I am sure I am none such.

IAGO

Do not weep, do not weep: — alas the day!

EMILIA

Hath she forsook so many noble matches,
Her father, and her country, and her friends,
To be call'd whore? would it not make one weep?

DESDEMONA

It is my wretched fortune.

IAGO

              Beshrew him for't!
How comes this trick upon him?

DESDEMONA

                      Nay, heaven doth know.

EMILIA

I will be hang'd, if some eternal villain,
Some busy and insinuating rogue,
Some cogging, cozening slave, to get some office,
Have not devis'd this slander; I'll be hang'd else.

IAGO

Fie, there is no such man; it is impossible.

DESDEMONA

If any such there be, heaven pardon him!

EMILIA

A halter pardon him! and hell gnaw his bones!
Why should he call her whore? who keeps her company?
What place? what time? what form? what likelihood?
The Moor's abus'd by some most villainous knave,
Some base notorious knave, some scurvy fellow: —
O heaven, that such companions thou'ldst unfold,
And put in every honest hand a whip
To lash the rascals naked through the world
Even from the east to th'west!

IAGO

                Speak within door.

EMILIA

O, fie upon them! Some such squire he was
That turn'd your wit the seamy side without,

And made you to suspect me with the Moor.

IAGO

You are a fool; go to.

DESDEMONA

     O good Iago,
What shall I do to win my lord again?
Good friend, go to him; for, by this light of heaven,
I know not how I lost him. Here I kneel: —
If e'er my will did trespass 'gainst his love,
Either in discourse of thought or actual deed;
Or that mine eyes, mine ears, or any sense,
Delighted them in any other form;
Or that I do not yet, and ever did,
And ever will — though he do shake me off
To beggarly divorcement — love him dearly,
Comfort forswear me! Unkindness may do much;
And his unkindness may defeat my life,
But never taint my love. I cannot say 'whore', —
It does abhor me now I speak the word;
To do the act that might the addition earn
Not the world's mass of vanity could make me.

IAGO

I pray you, be content; 'tis but his humour:
The business of the state does him offence,
And he does chide with you.

DESDEMONA

If 'twere no other, —

IAGO

    'Tis but so, I warrant.   *[Trumpets within.*
Hark, how these instruments summon to supper!
The messengers of Venice stay the meat:
Go in, and weep not; all things shall be well.

     [Exeunt DESDEMONA *and* EMILIA.
     Enter RODERIGO.

How now, Roderigo!

IAGO Go in, and weep not; all things shall be well.

RODERIGO

I do not find that thou deal'st justly with me.

IAGO

What in the contrary?

RODERIGO

Every day thou daff'st me with some device, Iago; and
rather, as it seems to me now, keep'st from me all
conveniency than suppliest me with the least advantage
of hope. I will, indeed, no longer endure it; nor am I yet
persuaded to put up in peace what already I have
foolishly suffer'd.

IAGO

Will you hear me, Roderigo?

RODERIGO

Faith, I have heard too much; for your words and
performances are no kin together.

IAGO

You charge me most unjustly.

RODERIGO

With naught but truth. I have wasted myself out of my
means. The jewels you have had from me to deliver to

Desdemona would half have corrupted a votarist: you
have told me she hath received them, and return'd me
expectations and comforts of sudden respect and
acquaintance; but I find none.

IAGO

Well; go to; very well.

RODERIGO

Very well! go to! I cannot go to, man; nor 'tis not very
well: nay, I think it is scurvy, and begin to find myself
fopp'd in it.

IAGO

Very well.

RODERIGO

I tell you 'tis not very well. I will make myself known to
Desdemona: if she will return me my jewels, I will give
over my suit, and repent my unlawful solicitation; if not,
assure yourself I will seek satisfaction of you.

IAGO

You have said now.

RODERIGO

Ay, and said nothing but what I protest intendment of
doing.

IAGO

Why, now I see there's mettle in thee; and even from
this instant to build on thee a better opinion than ever
before. Give me thy hand, Roderigo: thou hast taken
against me a most just exception; but yet, I protest, I
have dealt most directly in thy affair.

RODERIGO

It hath not appear'd.

IAGO

I grant, indeed, it hath not appear'd; and your suspicion
is not without wit and judgement. But, Roderigo, if thou
hast that in thee indeed, which I have greater reason to
believe now than ever, — I mean purpose, courage, and
valour, — this night show it: if thou the next night

following enjoy not Desdemona, take me from this
world with treachery, and devise engines for my life.

RODERIGO

Well, what is it? is it within reason and compass?

IAGO

Sir, there is especial commission come from Venice to
depute Cassio in Othello's place.

RODERIGO

Is that true? why, then Othello and Desdemona return
again to Venice.

IAGO

O, no; he goes into Mauritania, and takes away with him
the fair Desdemona, unless his abode be linger'd here by
some accident: wherein none can be so determinate as
the removing of Cassio.

RODERIGO

How do you mean, removing of him?

IAGO

Why, by making him uncapable of Othello's place, —
knocking out his brains.

RODERIGO

And that you would have me to do?

IAGO

Ay, if you dare do yourself a profit and a right. He sups
to-night with a harlotry, and thither will I go to him: —
he knows not yet of his honourable fortune. If you will
watch his going thence, — which I will fashion to fall
out between twelve and one, — you may take him at
your pleasure: I will be near to second your attempt, and
he shall fall between us. Come, stand not amazed at it,
but go along with me; I will show you such a necessity in
his death, that you shall think yourself bound to put it
on him. It is now high suppertime, and the night grows
to waste: about it.

RODERIGO

I will hear further reason for this.

IAGO

And you shall be satisfied.   [*Exeunt.*

SCENE III

Another room in the castle.

Enter OTHELLO, LODOVICO, DESDEMONA,
EMILIA, *and* ATTENDANTS.

LODOVICO

I do beseech you, sir, trouble yourself no further.

OTHELLO

O, pardon me; 'twill do me good to walk.

LODOVICO

Madam, good night; I humbly thank your ladyship.

DESDEMONA

Your honour is most welcome.

OTHELLO

                         Will you walk, sir?

O, — Desdemona, —

DESDEMONA

My lord?

OTHELLO

Get you to bed on th'instant: I will be return'd
forthwith: dismiss your attendant there: look't be done.

DESDEMONA

I will, my lord.

[*Exeunt* OTHELLO, LODOVICO, *and* ATTENDANTS.

EMILIA

How goes it now? he looks gentler than he did.

DESDEMONA

He says he will return incontinent:
He hath commanded me to go to bed,
And bade me to dismiss you.

EMILIA

                         Dismiss me!

DESDEMONA

It was his bidding; therefore, good Emilia,
Give me my nightly wearing, and adieu:
We must not now displease him.

EMILIA

I would you had never seen him!

DESDEMONA

So would not I: my love doth so approve him,
That even his stubbornness, his checks, his frowns, —
Prithee, unpin me, — have grace and favour in them.

EMILIA

I have laid those sheets you bade me on the bed.

DESDEMONA

All's one. — Good faith, how foolish are our minds! —
If I do die before thee, prithee, shroud me
In one of those same sheets.

EMILIA

           Come, come, you talk.

DESDEMONA

My mother had a maid call'd Barbara:
She was in love; and he she lov'd prov'd mad,
And did forsake her: she had a song of 'willow';
An old thing 'twas, but it express'd her fortune,
And she died singing it: that song to-night
Will not go from my mind; I have much to do,
But to go hang my head all at one side,
And sing it like poor Barbara. — Prithee, dispatch.

EMILIA

Shall I go fetch your night-gown?

DESDEMONA

           No, unpin me here. —
This Lodovico is a proper man.

EMILIA

A very handsome man.

DESDEMONA

He speaks well.

EMILIA

I know a lady in Venice would have walk'd barefoot to
Palestine for a touch of his nether lip.

DESDEMONA [*singing*].

    The poor soul sat sighing by a sycamore tree,
        Sing all a green willow;
    Her hand on her bosom, her head on her knee,
        Sing willow, willow, willow:
    The fresh streams ran by her, and murmur'd her
    moans;
        Sing willow, willow, willow;
    Her salt tears fell from her, and soften'd the
    stones; —

Lay by these: —
        Sing willow, willow, willow;
Prithee, hie thee; he'll come anon: —
        Sing all a green willow must be my garland.
        Let nobody blame him; his scorn I approve, —

Nay, that's not next. — Hark! who is't that knocks?

EMILIA

It is the wind.

DESDEMONA

    I call'd my love false love; but what said he then?
        Sing willow, willow, willow;
    If I court moe women, you'll couch with moe
    men: —

So, get thee gone; good night. Mine eyes do itch;
Doth that bode weeping?

EMILIA

                'Tis neither here nor there.

DESDEMONA

I have heard it said so. — O, these men, these men! —
Dost thou in conscience think, — tell me, Emilia, —
That there be women do abuse their husbands
In such gross kind?

EMILIA

           There be some such, no question.

DESDEMONA

Wouldst thou do such a deed for all the world?

EMILIA

Why, would not you?

DESDEMONA

                No, by this heavenly light!

EMILIA

Nor I neither by this heavenly light; I might do't as well
i'th'dark.

DESDEMONA

Wouldst thou do such a deed for all the world?

EMILIA

The world is a huge thing: it is a great price for a small
vice.

DESDEMONA

In troth, I think thou wouldst not.

EMILIA

In troth, I think I should; and undo't when I had done.
Marry, I would not do such a thing for a joint-ring, nor
for measures of lawn, nor for gowns, petticoats, nor
caps, nor any petty exhibition; but, for the whole world,
— why, who would not make her husband a cuckold to
make him a monarch? I should venture purgatory for't.

DESDEMONA

Beshrew me, if I would do such a wrong
For the whole world.

EMILIA

Why, the wrong is but a wrong i'th'world; and having
the world for your labour, 'tis a wrong in your own
world, and you might quickly make it right.

DESDEMONA

I do not think there is any such woman.

EMILIA

Yes, a dozen; and as many to th'vantage as would store
the world they play'd for.
But I do think it is their husbands' faults

If wives do fall: say that they slack their duties,
And pour our treasures into foreign laps;
Or else break out in peevish jealousies,
Throwing restraint upon us; or say they strike us,
Or scant our former having in despite;
Why, we have galls; and though we have some grace,
Yet have we some revenge. Let husbands know
Their wives have sense like them: they see, and smell,
And have their palates both for sweet and sour,
As husbands have. What is it that they do
When they change us for others? Is it sport?
I think it is: and doth affection breed it?
I think it doth: is't frailty that thus errs?
It is so too: — and have not we affections,
Desires for sport, and frailty, as men have?
Then let them use us well: else let them know,
The ills we do, their ills instruct us so.

DESDEMONA

Good night, good night: heaven me such usage send,
Not to pick bad from bad, but by bad mend!   [*Exeunt.*

ACT V

SCENE I

Cyprus. A street.

Enter IAGO *and* RODERIGO.

IAGO

Here, stand behind this bulk; straight will he come:
Wear thy good rapier bare, and put it home:
Quick, quick; fear nothing; I'll be at thy elbow:
It makes us, or it mars us; think on that,
And fix most firm thy resolution.

RODERIGO

Be near at hand; I may miscarry in't.

IAGO Here, stand behind this bulk; straight will he come.

IAGO
  Here, at thy hand: be bold, and take thy stand.
                                   [*Retires to a little distance.*
RODERIGO
  I have no great devotion to the deed;
  And yet he hath given me satisfying reasons: —
  'Tis but a man gone: — forth, my sword; he dies.
                                   [*Goes to his stand.*

IAGO

I have rubb'd this young quat almost to the sense,
And he grows angry. Now, whether he kill Cassio,
Or Cassio him, or each do kill the other,
Every way makes my gain: live Roderigo,
He calls me to a restitution large
Of gold and jewels that I bobb'd from him,
As gifts to Desdemona;
It must not be: if Cassio do remain,
He hath a daily beauty in his life
That makes me ugly; and, besides, the Moor
May unfold me to him; there stand I in much peril:
No, he must die. But so: I hear him coming.

Enter CASSIO.

RODERIGO

I know his gait, 'tis he. — Villain, thou diest!
          [Makes a pass at CASSIO.

CASSIO

That thrust had been mine enemy indeed,
But that my coat is better than thou know'st:
I will make proof of thine.
          [Draws, and wounds RODERIGO.

RODERIGO

          O, I am slain!
    *[*IAGO *cuts* CASSIO *behind in the leg, and exit.*

CASSIO

I am maim'd for ever. — Help, ho! murder! murder!
          [Falls.

Enter OTHELLO, *at some distance.*

OTHELLO

The voice of Cassio: — Iago keeps his word.

RODERIGO

O, villain that I am!

OTHELLO

          It is even so.

CASSIO

O, help, ho! light! a surgeon!

OTHELLO

'Tis he: — O brave Iago, honest and just,
That hast such noble sense of thy friend's wrong!
Thou teachest me: — Minion, your dear lies dead,
And your unblest fate hies: strumpet, I come!
Forth of my heart those charms, thine eyes, are blotted;
Thy bed lust-stain'd shall with lust's blood be spotted.

[*Exit.*

Enter LODOVICO *and* GRATIANO.

CASSIO

What, ho! no watch? no passage? murder! murder!

GRATIANO

'Tis some mischance; the cry is very direful.

CASSIO

O, help!

LODOVICO

Hark!

RODERIGO

O wretched villain!

LODOVICO

Two or three groan: — it is a heavy night:
These may be counterfeits: let's think't unsafe
To come in to the cry without more help.

RODERIGO

Nobody come? then shall I bleed to death.

LODOVICO

Hark!

GRATIANO

Here's one comes in his shirt, with light and weapons.

Enter IAGO, *with a light.*

IAGO

Who's there? whose noise is this that cries on murder?

LODOVICO

We do not know.

IAGO

Did not you hear a cry?

CASSIO

Here, here! for heaven's sake, help me!

IAGO

What's the matter?

GRATIANO

This is Othello's ancient, as I take it.

LODOVICO

The same indeed; a very valiant fellow.

IAGO

What are you here that cry so grievously?

CASSIO

Iago? O, I am spoil'd, undone by villains!
Give me some help.

IAGO

O me, lieutenant! what villains have done this?

CASSIO

I think that one of them is hereabout,
And cannot make away.

IAGO

O treacherous villains! —
What are you there? come in, and give some help.
                    [To LODOVICO and GRATIANO.

RODERIGO

O, help me here!

CASSIO

That's one of them.

IAGO

O murderous slave! O villain!
                    [Stabs RODERIGO.

RODERIGO

O damn'd Iago! O inhuman dog!

IAGO

Kill men i'th'dark! — Where be these bloody thieves? —
How silent is this town! — Ho! murder! murder! —
What may you be? are you of good or evil?

LODOVICO

As you shall prove us, praise us.

IAGO

Signior Lodovico?

LODOVICO

He, sir.

IAGO

I cry you mercy. Here's Cassio hurt by villains.

GRATIANO

Cassio!

IAGO

How is't, brother?

CASSIO

My leg is cut in two.

IAGO

Marry, heaven forbid! —
Light, gentlemen: — I'll bind it with my shirt.

Enter BIANCA.

BIANCA

What is the matter, ho? who is't that cried?

IAGO

Who is't that cried!

BIANCA

O my dear Cassio! my sweet Cassio!
O Cassio, Cassio, Cassio!

IAGO

O notable strumpet! — Cassio, may you suspect
Who they should be that have thus mangled you?

CASSIO

No.

GRATIANO

I am sorry to find you thus: I have been to seek you.

IAGO

Lend me a garter: — so. — O, for a chair,
To bear him easily hence!

BIANCA O my dear Cassio! my sweet Cassio!

BIANCA
Alas, he faints! — O Cassio, Cassio, Cassio!

IAGO
Gentlemen all, I do suspect this trash
To be a party in this injury. —
Patience awhile, good Cassio. — Come, come;
Lend me a light. — Know we this face or no?
Alas, my friend and my dear countryman
Roderigo? no: — yes, sure; O heaven! Roderigo.

GRATIANO
What, of Venice?

IAGO
Even he, sir: did you know him?

GRATIANO
                    Know him! ay.

IAGO
Signior Gratiano? I cry you gentle pardon;
These bloody accidents must excuse my manners
That so neglected you.

GRATIANO
                    I am glad to see you.

IAGO

How do you, Cassio? — O, a chair, a chair!

GRATIANO

Roderigo!

IAGO

He, he, 'tis he. — [*A chair brought in.*] O, that's well
    said; — the chair: —
Some good man bear him carefully from hence;
I'll fetch the general's surgeon. — [*to* BIANCA] For
    you, mistress,
Save you your labour. — He that lies slain here, Cassio,
Was my dear friend: what malice was between you?

CASSIO

None in the world; nor do I know the man.

IAGO [*to* BIANCA].

What, look you pale? — O, bear him out o'th'air. —
                    [*CASSIO and* RODERIGO *are borne off.*
Stay you, good gentlemen. — Look you pale, mistress? —
Do you perceive the gastness of her eye? —
Nay, if you stare, we shall hear more anon. —
Behold her well; I pray you, look upon her:
Do you see, gentlemen? nay, guiltiness will speak,
Though tongues were out of use.

Enter EMILIA.

EMILIA

'Las, what's the matter? what's the matter, husband?

IAGO

Cassio hath here been set on in the dark
By Roderigo, and fellows that are scap'd:
He's almost slain, and Roderigo dead.

EMILIA

Alas, good gentleman! alas, good Cassio!

IAGO

This is the fruit of whoring. — Prithee, Emilia,
Go know of Cassio where he supp'd to-night. —
[*to* BIANCA] What, do you shake at that?

BIANCA

He supp'd at my house; but I therefore shake not.

IAGO

O, did he so? I charge you, go with me.

EMILIA

Fie, fie upon thee, strumpet!

BIANCA

I am no strumpet; but of life as honest
As you that thus abuse me.

EMILIA

As I! foh! fie upon thee!

IAGO

Kind gentlemen, let's go see poor Cassio dress'd. —
[*to* BIANCA] Come, mistress, you must tell's another
tale. —
Emilia, run you to the citadel,
And tell my lord and lady what hath happ'd. —
Will you go on afore? — [*aside*] This is the night
That either makes me or fordoes me quite.   [*Exeunt.*

SCENE II

A bedchamber in the castle: DESDEMONA
in bed asleep; a light burning.

Enter OTHELLO.

OTHELLO

It is the cause, it is the cause, my soul, —
Let me not name it to you, you chaste stars!
It is the cause. — Yet I'll not shed her blood;
Nor scar that whiter skin of hers than snow,
And smooth as monumental alabaster.
Yet she must die, else she'll betray more men. —
Put out the light, and then put out the light:
If I quench thee, thou flaming minister,
I can again thy former light restore,
Should I repent me: — but once put out thy light,
Thou cunning'st pattern of excelling nature,

OTHELLO Put out the light, and then put out the light.

I know not where is that Promethean heat
That can thy light relume. When I have pluck'd the
rose,
I cannot give it vital growth again,
It needs must wither: — I'll smell it on the tree. —

[*Kissing her.*

O balmy breath, that dost almost persuade
Justice to break her sword! — One more, one more: —
Be thus when thou art dead, and I will kill thee,
And love thee after: — one more, and this the last:
So sweet was ne'er so fatal. I must weep,
But they are cruel tears: this sorrow's heavenly;
It strikes where it doth love. — She wakes.

DESDEMONA
Who's there? Othello?

OTHELLO
                    Ay, Desdemona.

DESDEMONA
Will you come to bed, my lord?

OTHELLO
Have you pray'd to-night, Desdemona?

DESDEMONA
                                        Ay, my lord.

OTHELLO
If you bethink yourself of any crime
Unreconcil'd as yet to heaven and grace,
Solicit for it straight.

DESDEMONA
Alack, my lord, what may you mean by that?

OTHELLO
Well, do it, and be brief; I will walk by:
I would not kill thy unprepared spirit;
No, — heaven forfend! — I would not kill thy soul.

DESDEMONA
Talk you of killing?

OTHELLO
Ay, I do.

DESDEMONA
Then heaven have mercy on me!

OTHELLO
Amen, with all my heart!

DESDEMONA

If you say so, I hope you will not kill me.

OTHELLO

Hum!

DESDEMONA

And yet I fear you; for you are fatal then
When your eyes roll so: why I should fear I know not,
Since guiltiness I know not; but yet I feel I fear.

OTHELLO

Think on thy sins.

DESDEMONA

They are loves I bear to you.

OTHELLO

Ay, and for that thou diest.

DESDEMONA

That death's unnatural that kills for loving. —
Alas, why gnaw you so your nether lip?
Some bloody passion shakes your very frame:
These are portents; but yet I hope, I hope,
They do not point on me.

OTHELLO

Peace, and be still.

DESDEMONA

I will so. What's the matter?

OTHELLO

That handkerchief which I so lov'd and gave thee
Thou gavest to Cassio.

DESDEMONA

No, by my life and soul!
Send for the man, and ask him.

OTHELLO

Sweet soul, take heed,
Take heed of perjury; thou art on thy death-bed.

DESDEMONA

Ay, but not yet to die.

OTHELLO

Yes, presently:

Therefore confess thee freely of thy sin;
For to deny each article with oath
Cannot remove nor choke the strong conception
That I do groan withal. Thou art to die.

DESDEMONA

Then Lord have mercy on me!

OTHELLO

              I say, amen.

DESDEMONA

And have you mercy too! — I never did
Offend you in my life; never lov'd Cassio
But with such general warranty of heaven
As I might love; I never gave him token.

OTHELLO

By heaven, I saw my handkerchief in's hand.
O perjured woman! thou dost stone my heart.
And mak'st me call what I intend to do
A murder, which I thought a sacrifice:
I saw the handkerchief.

DESDEMONA

         He found it, then;
I never gave it him: — send for him hither;
Let him confess a truth.

OTHELLO

         He hath confess'd.

DESDEMONA

What, my lord?

OTHELLO

That he hath us'd thee.

DESDEMONA

       How? unlawfully?

OTHELLO

                Ay.

DESDEMONA

He will not say so.

OTHELLO

       No, his mouth is stopp'd;

Honest Iago hath ta'en order for't.

DESDEMONA

O, my fear interprets: — what, is he dead?

OTHELLO

Had all his hairs been lives, my great revenge
Had stomach for them all.

DESDEMONA

Alas, he is betray'd, and I undone!

OTHELLO

Out, strumpet! weep'st thou for him to my face?

DESDEMONA

O, banish me, my lord, but kill me not!

OTHELLO

Down, strumpet!

DESDEMONA

Kill me to-morrow; let me live to-night!

OTHELLO

Nay, if you strive, —

DESDEMONA

But half an hour!

OTHELLO

     Being done, there is no pause.

DESDEMONA

But while I say one prayer!

OTHELLO

     It is too late. [*Smothers her.*

EMILIA [*at the door*].

My lord, my lord! what, ho! my lord, my lord!

OTHELLO

What noise is this? — Not dead? not yet quite dead?
I that am cruel am yet merciful;
I would not have thee linger in thy pain: —
So, so.

EMILIA [*within*].

What, ho! my lord, my lord!

OTHELLO

     Who's there?

EMILIA [*within*].

O, good my lord, I would speak a word with you!

OTHELLO

Yes: 'tis Emilia: — by and by. — She's dead. —
'Tis like she comes to speak of Cassio's death;
The noise was high. — Ha! no more moving?
Still as the grave. — Shall she come in? were't good? —
I think she stirs again: — no. — What's best to do?
If she come in, she'll sure speak to my wife:
My wife! my wife! what wife? I have no wife.
O, insupportable! O heavy hour!
Methinks it should be now a huge eclipse
Of sun and moon, and that th'affrighted globe
Should yawn at alteration.

EMILIA [*within*].

       I do beseech you
That I may speak with you, O, good my lord!

OTHELLO

I had forgot thee: O, come in, Emilia: —
Soft, — by and by: — let me the curtains draw. —
Where art thou?

           [*Opens the door.*

     Enter EMILIA.
  What's the matter with thee now?

EMILIA

O, my good lord, yonder's foul murders done!

OTHELLO

What, now?

EMILIA

But now, my lord.

OTHELLO

It is the very error of the moon;
She comes more near the earth than she was wont,
And makes men mad.

EMILIA

Cassio, my lord, hath kill'd a young Venetian
Call'd Roderigo.

OTHELLO
          Roderigo kill'd!
And Cassio kill'd!

EMILIA
          No, Cassio is not kill'd.

OTHELLO
Not Cassio kill'd! then murder's out of tune,
And sweet revenge grows harsh.

DESDEMONA
O falsely, falsely murder'd!

EMILIA
          Alas, what cry is that?

OTHELLO
That! what?

EMILIA
Out, and alas! that was my lady's voice. —
Help! help, ho! help! — O lady, speak again!
Sweet Desdemona! O sweet mistress, speak!

DESDEMONA
A guiltless death I die.

EMILIA
          O, who hath done
This deed?

DESDEMONA
       Nobody, — I myself. Farewell:
Commend me to my kind lord: O, farewell!   [*Dies.*

OTHELLO
Why, how should she be murder'd?

EMILIA
          Alas, who knows?

OTHELLO
You heard her say herself, it was not I.

EMILIA
She said so: I must needs report the truth.

OTHELLO
She's, like a liar, gone to burning hell:
'Twas I that kill'd her.

EMILIA

              O, the more angel she,
And you the blacker devil!

OTHELLO

She turn'd to folly, and she was a whore.

EMILIA

Thou dost belie her, and thou art a devil.

OTHELLO

She was false as water.

EMILIA

              Thou art rash as fire, to say
That she was false: O, she was heavenly true!

OTHELLO

Cassio did top her; ask thy husband else.
O, I were damn'd beneath all depth in hell,
But that I did proceed upon just grounds
To this extremity. Thy husband knew it all.

EMILIA

My husband!

OTHELLO

Thy husband.

EMILIA

That she was false to wedlock?

OTHELLO

Ay, with Cassio. Nay, had she been true,
If heaven would make me such another world
Of one entire and perfect chrysolite,
I'ld not have sold her for it.

EMILIA

My husband!

OTHELLO

         Ay, 'twas he that told me first:
An honest man he is, and hates the slime
That sticks on filthy deeds.

EMILIA

           My husband!

WILLIAM SHAKESPEARE

OTHELLO

What needs this iterance, woman? I say thy husband.

EMILIA

O mistress, villainy hath made mocks with love! —
My husband say that she was false!

OTHELLO

He, woman:
I say thy husband: dost understand the word?
My friend, thy husband, honest, honest Iago.

EMILIA

If he say so, may his pernicious soul
Rot half a grain a day! he lies to th'heart:
She was too fond of her most filthy bargain.

OTHELLO

Ha!

EMILIA

Do thy worst:
This deed of thine is no more worthy heaven
Than thou wast worthy her.

OTHELLO

Peace, you were best.

EMILIA

Thou hast not half that power to do me harm
As I have to be hurt. O gull! O dolt!
As ignorant as dirt! thou hast done a deed —
I care not for thy sword; I'll make thee known,
Though I lost twenty lives. — Help! help, ho! help!
The Moor hath kill'd my mistress! Murder! murder!

Enter MONTANO, GRATIANO, *and* IAGO.

MONTANO

What is the matter? — How now, general!

EMILIA

O, are you come, Iago? you have done well,
That men must lay their murders on your neck.

GRATIANO

What is the matter?

EMILIA

Disprove this villain, if thou be'st a man:
He says thou told'st him that his wife was false:
I know thou didst not, thou'rt not such a villain:
Speak, for my heart is full.

IAGO

I told him what I thought; and told no more
Than what he found himself was apt and true.

EMILIA

But did you ever tell him she was false?

IAGO

I did.

EMILIA

You told a lie; an odious, damned lie;
Upon my soul, a lie; a wicked lie: —
She false with Cassio! — did you say with Cassio?

IAGO

With Cassio, mistress. Go to, charm your tongue.

EMILIA

I will not charm my tongue; I am bound to speak:
My mistress here lies murder'd in her bed, —

ALL

O heavens forfend!

EMILIA

And your reports have set the murder on.

OTHELLO

Nay, stare not, masters: it is true, indeed.

GRATIANO

'Tis a strange truth.

MONTANO

O monstrous act!

EMILIA

Villainy, villainy, villainy!
I think upon't, — I think, — I smell't; — O villainy! —
I thought so then; — I'll kill myself for grief: —
O villainy, villainy!

IAGO

What, are you mad? I charge you, get you home.

EMILIA

Good gentlemen, let me have leave to speak:
'Tis proper I obey him, but not now. —
Perchance, Iago, I will ne'er go home.

OTHELLO

O! O! O!   [*Falling on the bed.*

EMILIA

                   Nay, lay thee down and roar;
For thou hast kill'd the sweetest innocent
That e'er did lift up eye.

OTHELLO

                          O, she was foul! —   [*Rising.*
I scarce did know you, uncle: there lies your niece,
Whose breath, indeed, these hands have newly stopp'd:
I know this act shows horrible and grim.

GRATIANO

Poor Desdemona! I am glad thy father's dead:
Thy match was mortal to him, and pure grief
Shore his old thread in twain: did he live now,
This sight would make him do a desperate turn,
Yea, curse his better angel from his side,
And fall to reprobance.

OTHELLO

'Tis pitiful; but yet Iago knows
That she with Cassio hath the act of shame
A thousand times committed; Cassio confess'd it:
And she did gratify his amorous works
With that recognisance and pledge of love
Which I first gave her; I saw it in his hand:
It was a handkerchief, an antique token
My father gave my mother.

EMILIA

O heaven! O heavenly powers!

IAGO

Come, hold your peace.

EMILIA

'Twill out, 'twill out: — I peace!
No, I will speak as liberal as the north:
Let heaven and men and devils, let them all,
All, all, cry shame against me, yet I'll speak.

IAGO

Be wise, and get you home.

EMILIA

I will not.
[IAGO *offers to stab* EMILIA.

GRATIANO

Fie!
Your sword upon a woman?

EMILIA

O thou dull Moor! that handkerchief thou speak'st of
I found by fortune, and did give my husband;
For often, with a solemn earnestness —
More than, indeed, belong'd to such a trifle —
He begg'd of me to steal it.

IAGO

Villainous whore!

EMILIA

She give it Cassio! no, alas, I found it,
And I did give't my husband.

IAGO

Filth, thou liest!

EMILIA

By heaven, I do not, I do not, gentlemen. —
O murderous coxcomb! what should such a fool
Do with so good a wife!

OTHELLO

Are there no stones in heaven
But what serve for the thunder? — Precious villain!
[*He runs at* IAGO: IAGO *stabs* EMILIA, *and exit.*

GRATIANO

The woman falls; sure, he hath kill'd his wife.

EMILIA

Ay, ay: — O, lay me by my mistress' side.

GRATIANO

He's gone, but his wife's kill'd.

MONTANO

'Tis a notorious villain. Take you this weapon,
Which I have here recover'd from the Moor:
Come, guard the door without; let him not pass,
But kill him rather. I'll after that same villain,
For 'tis a damned slave.

[*Exeunt* MONTANO *and* GRATIANO.

OTHELLO

             I am not valiant neither,
But every puny whipster gets my sword: —
But why should honour outlive honesty?
Let it go all.

EMILIA

        What did thy song bode, lady?
Hark, canst thou hear me? I will play the swan,
And die in music: — 'Willow, willow, willow. — '

                            [*Singing.*

Moor, she was chaste; she lov'd thee, cruel Moor;
So come my soul to bliss as I speak true;
So speaking as I think, I die, — I die.   [*Dies.*

OTHELLO

I have another weapon in this chamber;
It is a sword of Spain, the ice-brook's temper: —
O, here it is. — uncle, I must come forth.

GRATIANO [*within*].

If thou attempt it, it will cost thee dear:
Thou hast no weapon, and perforce must suffer.

OTHELLO

Look in upon me, then, and speak with me,
Or, naked as I am, I will assault thee.

            Enter GRATIANO.

GRATIANO

What is the matter?

OTHELLO
      Behold, I have a weapon;
A better never did itself sustain
Upon a soldier's thigh: I have seen the day
That, with this little arm and this good sword,
I have made my way through more impediments
Than twenty times your stop: — but, O vain boast!
Who can control his fate? 'tis not so now. —
Be not afraid, though you do see me weapon'd;
Here is my journey's end, here is my butt,
And very sea-mark of my utmost sail.
Do you go back dismay'd? 'tis a lost fear;
Man but a rush against Othello's breast,
And he retires: — where should Othello go? —
Now, how dost thou look now? O ill-starr'd wench!
Pale as thy smock! when we shall meet at compt,
This look of thine will hurl my soul from heaven,
And fiends will snatch at it. Cold, cold, my girl!
Even like thy chastity. —
O cursed, cursed slave! — whip me, ye devils,
From the possession of this heavenly sight!
Blow me about in winds! roast me in sulphur!
Wash me in steep-down gulfs of liquid fire! —
O Desdemona! Desdemona! dead!
O! O! O!

Enter LODOVICO, MONTANO, CASSIO *carried in a*
  chair, and OFFICERS *with* IAGO, *prisoner.*

LODOVICO
Where is this rash and most unfortunate man?

OTHELLO
That's he that was Othello; — here I am.

LODOVICO
Where is that viper? bring the villain forth.

OTHELLO
I look down towards his feet, — but that's a fable.
If that thou be'st a devil, I cannot kill thee.

        [*Wounds* IAGO.

LODOVICO

Wrench his sword from him.   [OTHELLO *is disarm'd.*

IAGO

I bleed, sir; but not kill'd.

OTHELLO

I am not sorry neither: I'ld have thee live;
For, in my sense, 'tis happiness to die.

LODOVICO

O thou Othello, that wert once so good,
Fall'n in the practice of a damned slave,
What shall be said to thee?

OTHELLO

Why, any thing:
An honourable murderer, if you will;
For naught I did in hate, but all in honour.

LODOVICO

This wretch hath part confess'd his villainy:
Did you and he consent in Cassio's death?

OTHELLO

Ay.

CASSIO

Dear general, I never gave you cause.

OTHELLO

I do believe it, and I ask your pardon.
Will you, I pray, demand that demi-devil
Why he hath thus ensnared my soul and body?

IAGO

Demand me nothing: what you know, you know:
From this time forth I never will speak word.

LODOVICO

What, not to pray?

GRATIANO

Torments will ope your lips.

OTHELLO

Well, thou dost best.

LODOVICO

Sir, you shall understand what hath befall'n,

Which, as I think, you know not. Here is a letter
Found in the pocket of the slain Roderigo;
And here another: the one of them imports
The death of Cassio to be undertook
By Roderigo.

OTHELLO
O villain!

CASSIO
Most heathenish and most gross!

LODOVICO
Now here's another discontented paper,
Found in his pocket too; and this, it seems,
Roderigo meant t'have sent this damned villain;
But that, belike, Iago in the interim
Came in and satisfied him.

OTHELLO
O the pernicious caitiff! —
How came you, Cassio, by that handkerchief
That was my wife's?

CASSIO
I found it in my chamber:
And he himself confess'd but even now
That there he dropp'd it for a special purpose
Which wrought to his desire.

OTHELLO
O fool! fool! fool!

CASSIO
There is besides in Roderigo's letter, —
How he upbraids Iago, that he made him
Brave me upon the watch; whereon it came
That I was cast: and even but now he spake,
After long seeming dead, — Iago hurt him,
Iago set him on.

LODOVICO
You must forsake this room, and go with us:
Your power and your command is taken off,
And Cassio rules in Cyprus. For this slave,

If there be any cunning cruelty
That can torment him much and hold him long,
It shall be his. You shall close prisoner rest,
Till that the nature of your fault be known
To the Venetian state. — Come, bring him away.

OTHELLO

Soft you; a word or two before you go.
I have done the state some service, and they know't; —
No more of that. — I pray you, in your letters,
When you shall these unlucky deeds relate,
Speak of me as I am; nothing extenuate,
Nor set down aught in malice: then must you speak
Of one that lov'd not wisely, but too well;
Of one not easily jealous, but, being wrought,
Perplex'd in the extreme; of one whose hand,
Like the base Indian, threw a pearl away
Richer than all his tribe; of one whose subdued eyes,
Albeit unused to the melting mood,
Drop tears as fast as the Arabian trees
Their medicinable gum. Set you down this;
And say besides, that in Aleppo once,
Where a malignant and a turban'd Turk
Beat a Venetian and traduc'd the state,
I took by th'throat the circumcised dog,
And smote him — thus.   [*He stabs himself.*

LODOVICO

O bloody period!

GRATIANO

                    All that's spoke is marr'd.

OTHELLO

I kiss'd thee ere I kill'd thee: no way but this,
                    [*Falling upon* DESDEMONA.
Killing myself, to die upon a kiss.   [*Dies.*

CASSIO

This did I fear, but thought he had no weapon;
For he was great of heart.

LODOVICO [*to* IAGO].
                  O Spartan dog,
More fell than anguish, hunger, or the sea!
Look on the tragic loading of this bed;
This is thy work: the object poisons sight;
Let it be hid. Gratiano, keep the house,
And seize upon the fortunes of the Moor,
For they succeed on you. To you, lord governor,
Remains the censure of this hellish villain;
The time, the place, the torture. O, enforce it!
Myself will straight aboard, and to the state
This heavy act with heavy heart relate.   [*Exeunt.*

GLOSSARY

References are given only for words having more than one meaning, the first use of each sense being then noted.

Abate, *v.t.* to diminish. M.N.D. III. 2. 432. Deduct, except. L.L.L. v. 2. 539. Cast down. Cor. III. 3. 134. Blunt. R III. v. 5. 35. Deprive. Lear, II. 4. 159.

Abatement, *sb.* diminution Lear, I. 4. 59. Depreciation. Tw.N. I. 1. 13.

Abjects, *sb.* outcasts, servile persons.

Able, *v.t.* to warrant.

Abode, *v.t.* to forebode. 3 H VI. V. 6. 45.

Abode, *sb.* stay, delay. M. of V. II. 6. 77.

Abodements, *sb.* forebodings.

Abram, *adj.* auburn.

Abridgement, *sb.* short entertainment, for pastime.

Abrook, *v.t.* to brook, endure.

Absey book, *sb.* ABC book, or primer.

Absolute, *adj.* resolved. M. for M. III. 1. 5. Positive. Cor. III. 2. 39. Perfect. H V. III. 7. 26. Complete. Tp. I. 2. 109; Lucr. 853.

Aby, *v.t.* to atone for, expiate.

Accite, *v.t.* to cite, summon.

Acknown, *adj.* cognisant.

Acture, *sb.* performance.

Addition, *sb.* title, attribute.

Adoptious, *adj.* given by adoption.

Advice, *sb.* consideration.

Aery, *sb.* eagle's nest or brood. R III. I. 3. 265, 271. Hence generally any brood. Ham. II. 2. 344.

Affectioned, *p.p.* affected.

Affeered, *p.p.* sanctioned, confirmed.

Affiance, *sb.* confidence, trust.

Affined, *p.p.* related. T. & C. I. 3. 25. Bound. Oth. I. 1. 39.

Affront, *v.t.* to confront, meet.

147

Affy, *v.t.* to betroth. 2 H VI. IV . I. 80. *v.t.* to trust. T.A. I.I. 47.

Aglet-baby, *sb.* small figure cut on the tag of a lace (Fr. *aiguillette*). T. of S. I. 2. 78.

Agnize, *v.t.* to acknowledge, confess.

Agood, *adv.* much.

Aim, *sb.* a guess.

Aim, to cry aim, to encourage, an archery term.

Alderliefest, *adj.* most loved of all.

Ale, *sb.* alehouse.

All amort, completely dejected (Fr. *a la mort*).

Allicholy, *sb.* melancholy.

Allow, *v.t.* to approve.

Allowance, *sb.* acknowledgement, approval.

Ames-ace, *sb.* the lowest throw of the dice.

Anchor, *sb.* anchorite, hermit.

Ancient, *sb.* ensign, standard. I H IV. IV. 2. 32. Ensign, ensign-bearer. I H IV. IV. 2. 24.

Ancientry, *sb.* antiquity, used of old people, W.T. III. 3. 62. Of the gravity which belongs to antiquity, M.A. II. I. 75.

Angel, *sb.* gold coin, worth about Ios.

Antic, *adj.* fantastic. Ham. I. 5. 172.

Antick, *v.t.* to make a buffoon of. A. & C. II. 7. 126.

Antick, *sb.* buffoon of the old plays.

Appeal, *sb.* impeachment.

Appeal, *v.t.* to impeach.

Apperil, *sb.* peril.

Apple-john, *sb.* a shrivelled winter apple.

Argal, corruption of the Latin *ergo*, therefore.

Argo, corruption of *ergo*, therefore.

Aroint thee, begone, get thee gone.

Articulate, *v.i.* to make articles of peace. Cor. I. 9. 75. *v.t.* to set forth in detail. I H IV. V. I. 72.

Artificial, *adj.* working by art.

Askance, *v.t.* to make look askance or sideways, make to avert.

Aspic, *sb.* asp.

Assured, *p.p.* betrothed.

Atone, *v.t.* to reconcile. R II. I. I. 202. Agree. As V. 4. 112.

Attorney, *sb.* proxy, agent.

Attorneyed, *p.p.* done by proxy. W T. I. 1. 28. Engaged as an attorney, M. for M. V. 1. 383.

Attribute, *sb.* reputation.

Avail, *sb.* profit.

Avise, *v.t.* to inform. Are you avised? = Do you know?

Awful, *adj.* filled with regard for authority.

Awkward, *adj.* contrary.

Baby, *sb.* a doll.

Baccare, go back, a spurious Latin word.

Back-trick, a caper backwards in dancing.

Baffle, *v.t.* to disgrace (a recreant knight).

Bale, *sb.* evil, mischief.

Ballow, *sb.* cudgel.

Ban, *v.t.* curse. 2 H VI. II. 4. 25. *sb.* a curse. Ham. III. 2. 269.

Band, *sb.* bond.

Bank, *v.t.* sail along the banks of.

Bare, *v.t.* to shave.

Barn, *v.t.* to put in a barn.

Barn, or Barne, *sb.* bairn, child.

Base, *sb.* a rustic game. Bid the base = Challenge to a race. Two G. I. 2. 97.

Bases, *sb.* knee-length skirts worn by mounted knights.

Basilisco-like, Basilisco, a character in the play of *Soliman and Perseda*.

Basilisk, *sb.* a fabulous serpent. H V. V. 2. 17. A large cannon. 1 H IV. II. 3. 57.

Bate, *sb.* strife.

Bate, *v.i.* flutter as a hawk. 1 H IV. IV. 1. 99. Diminish. 1 H IV. III. 3. 2.

Bate, *v.t.* abate. Tp. I. 2. 250. Beat down, weaken. M. of V. III. 3. 32.

Bavin, *adj.* made of bavin or brushwood. 1 H IV. III. 2. 61.

Bawbling, *adj.* trifling, insignificant.

Baw-cock, *sb.* fine fellow (Fr. *beau coq.*) H V. III. 2. 25.

Bay, *sb.* space between the main timbers in a roof.

Beadsman, *sb.* one who is hired to offer prayers for another.

Bearing-cloth, *sb.* the cloth in which a child was carried to be christened.

Bear in hand, to deceive with false hopes.

Beat, *v.i.* to meditate. 2 H IV. II. I. 20. Throb. Lear, III. 4. 14.

Becoming, *sb.* grace.

Beetle, *sb.* a heavy mallet, 2 H IV. I. 2. 235. Beetle-headed = heavy, stupid. T. of S. IV. I. 150.

Behave, *v.t.* to control.

Behest, *sb.* command.

Behove, *sb.* behoof.

Be-lee'd, *p.p.* forced to lee of the wind.

Bench, *v.i.* to seat on the bench of justice. Lear, III. 6. 38. *v.t.* to elevate to the bench. W.T. I .2. 313.

Bench-hole, the hole of a privy.

Bergomask, a rustic dance, named from Bergamo in Italy.

Beshrew, *v.t.* to curse; but not used seriously.

Besort, *v.t.* to fit, suit.

Bestraught, *adj.* distraught.

Beteem, *v.t.* to permit, grant.

Bezonian, *sb.* a base and needy fellow.

Bias, *adj.* curving like the bias side of a bowling bowl.

Biggen, *sb.* a nightcap.

Bilbo, *sb.* a Spanish rapier, named from Bilbao or Bilboa.

Bilboes, *sb.* stocks used for punishment on shipboard.

Birdbolt, *sb.* a blunt-headed arrow used for birds.

Bisson, *adj.* dim-sighted. Cor. II. I. 65. Bisson rheum = blinding tears. Ham. II. 2. 514.

Blacks, *sb.* black mourning clothes.

Blank, *sb.* the white mark in the centre of a target.

Blank, *v.t.* to blanch, make pale.

Blanks, *sb.* royal charters left blank to be filled in as occasion dictated.

Blench, *sb.* a swerve, inconsistency.

Blistered, *adj.* padded out, puffed.

Block, *sb.* the wood on which hats are made. M.A. I. I. 71. Hence, the style of hat. Lear, IV. 6. 185.

Blood-boltered, *adj.* clotted with blood.

Blowse, *sb.* a coarse beauty.

Bob, *sb.* smart rap, jest.

Bob, *v.t.* to beat hard, thwack. R III. V. 3. 335. To obtain by fraud, cheat. T. & C. III. 1. 69.

Bodge, *v.i.* to budge.

Bodkin, *sb.* small dagger, stiletto.

Boggle, *v.i.* to swerve, shy, hesitate.

Boggler, *sb.* swerver.

Boln, *adj.* swollen.

Bolt, *v.t.* to sift, refine.

Bolter, *sb.* a sieve.

Bombard, *sb.* a leathern vessel for liquor.

Bona-robas, *sb.* flashily dressed women of easy virtue.

Bonnet, *v.i.* to doff the hat, be courteous.

Boot, *sb.* profit. 1 H VI. IV. 6. 52. That which is given over and above. R III. IV. 4. 65. Booty. 3 H VI. IV. 1. 13.

Boots, *sb.* Give me not the boots = do not inflict on me the torture of the boots, which were employed to wring confessions.

Bosky, *adj.* woody.

Botcher, *sb.* patcher of old clothes.

Bots, *sb.* small worms in horses.

Bottled, *adj.* big-bellied.

Brabble, *sb.* quarrel, brawl.

Brabbler, *sb.* a brawler.

Brach, *sb.* a hound-bitch.

Braid, *adj.* deceitful.

Braid, *v.t.* to upbraid, reproach.

Brain, *v.t.* to conceive in the brain.

Brazed, *p.p.* made like brass, perhaps hardened in the fire.

Breeched, *p.p.* as though wearing breeches. Mac. II. 3. 120.

Breeching, *adj.* liable to be breeched for a flogging.

Breese, *sb.* a gadfly.

Brib'd-buck, *sb.* perhaps a buck distributed in presents.

Brock, *sb.* badger.

Broken, *adj.* of a mouth with some teeth missing.

Broker, *sb.* agent, go-between.

Brownist, a follower of Robert Brown, the founder of the sect of Independents.

Buck, *v.t.* to wash and beat linen.

Buck-basket, *sb.* a basket to take linen to be bucked.

Bucking, *sb.* washing.

Buckle, *v.i.* to encounter hand to hand, cope. 1. H VI. I. 2. 95. To bow. 2 H VI. I. 1. 141.

Budget, *sb.* a leather scrip or bag.

Bug, *sb.* bugbear, a thing causing terror.

Bugle, *sb.* a black bead.

Bully, *sb.* a fine fellow.

Bully-rook, *sb.* a swaggering cheater.

Bung, *sb.* pickpocket.

Burgonet, *sb.* close-fitting Burgundian helmet.

Busky, *adj.* woody.

By-drinkings, *sb.* drinks taken between meals.

Caddis, *sb.* worsted trimming, galloon.

Cade, *sb.* cask, barrel.

Caitiff, *sb.* captive, slave, a wretch. *adj.* R II. I. 2. 53.

Caliver, *sb.* musket.

Callet, *sb.* trull, drab.

Calling, *sb.* appellation.

Calm, *sb.* qualm.

Canaries = quandary.

Canary, *sb.* a lively Spanish dance. *v.i.* to dance canary.

Canker, *sb.* the dog-rose or wild-rose. 1 H IV. I. 3. 176. A worm that destroys blossoms. M.N.D. II. 2.3.

Canstick, *sb.* candlestick.

Cantle, *sb.* piece, slice.

Canton, *sb.* canto.

Canvass, *v.t.* shake as in a sieve, take to task.

Capable, *adj.* sensible. As III. 5. 23. Sensitive, susceptible. Ham. III. 4. 128. Comprehensive. Oth. III. 3. 459. Able to possess. Lear, II. 1. 85.

Capocchia, *sb.* the feminine of capocchio (Ital.), simpleton.

Capriccio, *sb.* caprice, fancy.

Captious, *adj.* either a contraction of capacious or a coined word meaning capable of receiving.

Carack, *sb.* a large merchant ship.

Carbonado, *sb.* meat scotched for boiling. *v.t.* to hack like a carbonado.

Card, *sb.* a cooling card = a sudden and decisive stroke.

Card, *v.t.* to mix (liquids).

Cardecu, *sb.* quarter of a French crown (*quart d'écu*).

Care, *v.i.* to take care.

Careire, career, *sb.* a short gallop at full speed.

Carlot, *sb.* peasant.

Carpet consideration, On, used of those made knights for court services, not for valour in the field.

Carpet-mongers, *sb.* carpet-knights.

Carpets, *sb.* tablecloths.

Case, *v.t.* to strip off the case or skin of an animal. A.W. III. 6. 103. Put on a mask. 1 H IV. II. 2. 55.

Case, *sb.* skin of an animal. Tw.N. V. 1.163. A set, as of musical instruments, which were in fours. H V. III. 2. 4.

Cashiered, *p.p.* discarded; in M.W.W. I. 1. 168 it probably means relieved of his cash.

Cataian, *sb.* a native of Cathay, a Chinaman; a cant word.

Cater-cousins, good friends.

Catlings, *sb.* catgut strings for musical instruments.

Cautel, *sb.* craft, deceit, stratagem.

Cautelous, *adj.* crafty, deceitful.

Ceased, *p.p.* put off.

Censure, *sb.* opinion, judgement.

Certify, *v.t.* to inform, make certain.

Cess, *sb.* reckoning; out of all cess = immoderately.

Cesse = cease.

Champain, *sb.* open country.

Channel, *sb.* gutter.

Chape, *sb.* metal end of a scabbard.

Chapless, *adj.* without jaws.

Charact, *sb.* a special mark or sign of office.

Chare, *sb.* a turn of work.

Charge, *sb.* weight, importance. W.T. IV. 3. 258. Cost, expense. John I. 1. 49.

Chaudron, *sb.* entrails.

Check, *sb.* rebuke, reproof.

Check, *v.t.* to rebuke, chide.

Check, *v.i.* to start on sighting game.

Cherry-pit, *sb.* a childish game consisting of pitching cherry-stones into a small hole.

Cheveril, *sb.* leather of kid skin. R. & J. II. 3. 85. *adj.* Tw.N. III. 1. 12.

Che vor ye = I warn you.

Chewet, *sb.* chough. 1 H IV. V. 1. 29. (Fr. *chouette* or *chutte*). Perhaps with play on other meaning of chewet, *i.e.*, a kind of meat pie.

Childing, *adj.* fruitful.

Chop, *v.t.* to clop, pop.

Chopine, *sb.* shoe with a high sole.

Choppy, *adj.* chapped.

Christendom, *sb.* Christian name.

Chuck, *sb.* chick, term of endearment.

Chuff, *sb.* churl, boor.

Cinque pace, *sb.* a slow stately dance. M.A. II. 1. 72. Compare sink-a-pace in Tw.N. I. 3. 126.

Cipher, *v.t.* to decipher.

Circumstance, *sb.* particulars, details. Two G. I. 1. 36. Ceremonious phrases. M. of V. I. 1. 154.

Circumstanced, *p.p.* swayed by circumstance.

Citizen, *adj.* town-bred, effeminate.

Cittern, *sb.* guitar.

Clack-dish, *sb.* wooden dish carried by beggars.

Clamour, *v.t.* to silence.

Clapper-claw, *v.t.* to thrash, drub.

Claw, *v.t.* to scratch, flatter.

Clepe, *v.t.* to call.

Cliff, *sb.* clef, the key in music.

Cling, *v.t.* to make shrivel up.

Clinquant, *adj.* glittering with gold or silver lace or decorations.

Close, *sb.* cadence in music. R II. II. 1. 12. *adj.* secret. T. of S. Ind. I. 127. *v.i.* to come to an agreement, make terms. Two G. II. 5. 12.

Closely, *adv.* secretly.

Clout, *sb.* bull's-eye of a target.

Clouted, *adj.* hobnailed (others explain as patched).

Cobloaf, *sb.* a crusty, ill-shapen loaf.

Cockered, *p.p.* pampered.

Cockle, *sb.* the corncockle weed.

Cockney, *sb.* a city-bred person, a foolish wanton.

Cock-shut time, *sb.* twilight.

Codding, *adj.* lascivious.

Codling, *sb.* an unripe apple.

Cog, *v.i.* to cheat. R III I. 3. 48. *v.t.* to get by cheating, filch. Cor. III. 2. 133.

Coistrel, *sb.* groom.

Collection, *sb.* inference.

Collied, *p.p.* blackened, darkened.

Colour, *sb.* pretext. Show no colour, or bear no colour = allow of no excuse.

Colours, fear no colours = fear no enemy, be afraid of nothing.

Colt, *v.t.* to make a fool of, gull.

Combinate, *adj.* betrothed.

Combine, *v.t.* to bind.

Comfect, *sb.* comfit.

Commodity, *sb.* interest, advantage. John, II. 1. 573. Cargo of merchandise. Tw.N. III. 1. 46.

Comparative, *adj.* fertile in comparisons. 1 H IV. I. 2. 83.

Comparative, *sb.* a rival in wit. 1 H IV. III. 2. 67.

Compassed, *adj.* arched, round.

Complexion, *sb.* temperament.

Comply, *v.i.* to be ceremonious.

Composition, *sb.* agreement, consistency.

Composture, *sb.* compost.

Composure, *sb.* composition. T. & C. II. 3. 238; A. & C. I. 4. 22. Compact. T. & C. II. 3. 100.

Compt. *sb.* account, reckoning.

Comptible, *adj.* susceptible, sensitive.

Con, *v.t.* to study, learn; con thanks = give thanks.

Conceptious, *adj.* apt at conceiving.

Conclusion, *sb.* experiment.

Condolement, *sb.* lamentation. Ham. I. 2. 93. Consolation, Per. II. 1. 150.

Conduce, *v.i.* perhaps to tend to happen.

Conduct, *sb.* guide, escort.

Confiners, *sb.* border peoples.

Confound, *v.t.* to waste. 1 H IV. I. 3. 100. Destroy. M. of V. III. 2. 278.

Congied, *p.p.* taken leave (Fr. *congé*).

Consent, *sb.* agreement, plot.

Consist, *v.i.* to insist.

Consort, *sb.* company, fellowship. Two G. III. 2. 84; IV. 1. 64. *v.t.* to accompany. C. of E. I. 2. 28.

Conspectuity, *sb.* power of vision.

Constant, *adj.* consistent.

Constantly, *adv.* firmly, surely.

Conster, *v.t.* to construe, interpret.

Constringed, *p.p.* compressed.

Consul, *sb.* senator.

Containing, *sb.* contents.

Contraction, *sb.* the making of the marriage-contract.

Contrive, *v.t.* to wear out, spend. T. of S. I. 2. 273. Conspire. J.C. II. 3. 16.

Control, *v.t.* to check, contradict.

Convent, *v.t.* to summon.

Convert, *v.i.* to change.

Convertite, *sb.* a penitent.

Convince, *v.t.* to overcome. Mac. I. 7. 64. Convict. T. & C. II. 2. 130.

Convive, *v.i.* to banquet together.

Convoy, *sb.* conveyance, escort.

Copatain hat, *sb.* a high-crowned hat.

Cope, *v.t.* to requite. M. of V. IV. 1. 412.

Copesmate, *sb.* a companion.

Copped, *adj.* round-topped.

Copulatives, *sb.* persons desiring to be coupled in marriage.

Copy, *sb.* theme, text. C. of E. V. 1. 62. Tenure. Mac. III. 2. 37.

Coranto, *sb.* a quick, lively dance.

Corky, *adj.* shrivelled (with age).

Cornet, *sb.* a band of cavalry.

Corollary, *sb.* a supernumerary.

Cosier, *sb.* botcher, cobbler.

Costard, *sb.* an apple, the head (slang).

Cote, *v.t.* to come up with, pass on the way.

Cot-quean, *sb.* a man who busies himself in women's affairs.

Couch, *v.t.* to make to cower.

Counter, *adv.* to run or hunt counter is to trace the scent of the game backwards.

Counter, *sb.* a metal disk used in reckoning.

Counter-caster, *sb.* one who reckons by casting up counters.

Countermand, *v.t.* to prohibit, keep in check. C. of E. IV. 2. 37. Contradict. Lucr. 276.

Countervail, *v.t.* to outweigh.

County, *sb.* count. As II. 1. 67.

Couplet, *sb.* a pair.

Courser's hair, a horse's hair laid in water was believed to turn into a serpent.

Court holy-water, *sb.* flattery.

Courtship, *sb.* courtly manners.

Convent, *sb.* a convent.

Cox my passion = God's passion.

Coy, *v.t.* to fondle, caress. M.N.D. IV. 1. 2. *v.i.* to disdain. Cor. V. 1. 6.

Crack, *v.i.* to boast. *sb.* an urchin.

Crank, *sb.* winding passage. *v.i.* to wind, twist.

Crants, *sb.* garland, chaplet.

Crare, *sb.* a small sailing vessel.

Crisp, *adj.* curled.

Cross, *sb.* a coin (stamped with a cross).

Cross-row, *sb.* alphabet.

Crow-keeper, *sb.* a boy, or scare-crow, to keep crows from corn.

Cullion, *sb.* a base fellow.

Cunning, *sb.* knowledge, skill. *adj.* knowing, skilful, skilfully wrought.

Curb, *v.i.* to bow, cringe obsequiously.

Curdied, *p.p.* congealed.

Curiosity, *sb.* scrupulous nicety.

Curst, *adj.* bad-tempered.

Curtal, *adj.* having a docked tail. *sb.* a dock-tailed horse.

Customer, *sb.* a loose woman.

Cut, *sb.* a bobtailed horse.

Cuttle, *sb.* a bully.

Daff, *v.t.* to doff. Daff aside = thrust aside slightingly.

Darraign, *v.t.* to arrange, order the ranks for battle.

Dash, *sb.* mark of disgrace.

Daubery, *sb.* false pretence, cheat.

Day-woman, *sb.* dairy-woman.

Debosht, *p.p.* debauched.

Deck, *sb.* pack of cards.

Deem, *sb.* doom; opinion.

Defeat, *v.t.* to disguise. Oth. I. 3. 333. Destroy. Oth. IV. 2. 160.

Defeature, *sb.* disfigurement.

Defend, *v.t.* to forbid.

Defuse, *v.t.* to disorder and make unrecognizable.

Defused, *p.p.* disordered, shapeless.

Demerit, *sb.* desert.

Denier, *sb.* a small French coin.

Dern, *adj.* secret, dismal.

Detect, *v.t.* to discover, disclose.

Determinate, *p.p.* determined upon. Tw.N. II. I. 10. Decided. Oth. IV. 2. 229. Ended. Sonn. LXXXVII. 4. *v.t.* bring to an end. R II. I. 3.

Dich, *v.i.* do to, happen to.

Diet, *v.t.* keep strictly, as if by a prescribed regimen.

Diffidence, *sb.* distrust, suspicion.

Digression, *sb.* transgression.

Diminutives, *sb.* the smallest of coins.

Directitude, *sb.* a blunder for some word unknown. Cor. IV. 5. 205.

Disanimate, *v.t.* to discourage.

Disappointed, *p.p.* unprepared.

Discandy, *v.i.* to thaw, melt.

Discipled, *p.p.* taught.

Disclose, *v.t.* to hatch. *sb.* the breaking of the shell by the chick on hatching.

Disme, *sb.* a tenth.

Distain, *v.t.* to stain, pollute.

Dive-dapper, *sb.* dabchick.

Dividant, *adj.* separate, different.

Dotant, *sb.* dotard.

Doubt, *sb.* fear, apprehension.

Dout, *v.t.* to extinguish.

Dowlas, *sb.* coarse linen.

Dowle, *sb.* down, the soft plumage of a feather.

Down-gyved, *adj.* hanging down about the ankle like gyves.

Dribbling, *adj.* weakly shot.

Drugs, *sb.* drudges.

Drumble, *v.i.* to be sluggish or clumsy.

Dry-beat, *v.t.* to cudgel, thrash.

Dry-foot. To draw dry-foot, track by scent.

Dudgeon, *sb.* the handle of a dagger.

Due, *v.t.* to endue.

Dump, *sb.* a sad strain.

Dup, *v.t.* to open.

Ean, *v.i.* to yean, lamb.

Ear, *v.t.* to plough, till.

Eche, *v.t.* to eke out.

Eftest, *adv.* readiest.

Eftsoons, *adv.* immediately.

Egal, *adj.* equal.

Egally, *adv.* equally.

Eisel, *sb.* vinegar.

Elf, *v.t.* to mat hair in a tangle; believed to be the work of elves.

Emballing, *sb.* investiture with the crown and sceptre.

Embarquement, *sb.* hindrance, restraint.

Ember-eyes, *sb.* vigils of Ember days.

Embowelled, *p.p.* emptied, exhausted.

Emmew, *v.t.* perhaps to mew up.

Empiricutic, *adj.* empirical, quackish.

Emulation, *sb.* jealous rivalry.

Enacture, *sb.* enactment, performance.

Encave, *v.t.* to hide, conceal.

Encumbered, *p.p.* folded.

End, *sb.* still an end = continually.

End, *v.t.* to get in the harvest.

Englut, *v.t.* to swallow.

Enlargement, *sb.* liberty, liberation.

Enormous, *adj.* out of the norm, monstrous.

Enseamed, *p.p.* defiled, filthy.

Ensear, *v.t.* to sear up, make dry.

Enshield, *adj.* enshielded, protected.

Entertain, *v.t.* to take into one's service.

Entertainment, *sb.* service.

Entreat, *v.t.* to treat.

Entreatments, *sb.* invitations.

Ephesian, *sb.* boon companion.

Eryngoes, *sb.* roots of the sea-holly, a supposed aphrodisiac.

Escot, *v.t.* to pay for.

Espial, *sb.* a spy.

Even Christian, *sb.* fellow Christian.

Excrement, *sb.* anything that grows out of the body, as hair, nails, etc. Used of the beard. M. of V. III. 2. 84. Of the hair. C. of E. II. 2. 79. Of the moustache. L.L.L. V. I. 98.

Exhibition, *sb.* allowance, pension.

Exigent, *sb.* end. 1 H VI. II. 5. 9. Exigency, critical need. J. C. V. 1. 19.

Exion, *sb.* blunder for action.

Expiate, *v.t* . to terminate. Sonn. XXII. 4.

Expiate, *p.p.* ended. R III. III. 3. 24.

Exsufflicate, *adj.* inflated, both literally and metaphorically.

Extent, *sb.* seizure. As III. 1. 17. Violent attack. Tw.N. IV. 1. 51. Condescension, favour. Ham. II. 2. 377. Display. T. A. IV. 4. 3.

Extraught, *p.p.* extracted.

Extravagancy, *sb.* vagrancy, aimless wandering about.

Eyas, *sb.* a nestling, a young hawk just taken from the nest.

Eyas-musket, *sb.* the young sparrow-hawk.

Eye, *v.i.* to appear, look to the eye.

Facinerious, *adj.* wicked.

Fadge, *v.i.* to succeed, suit.

Fading, *sb.* the burden of a song.

Fair, *v.t.* to make beautiful.

Fairing, *sb.* a gift.

Faitor, *sb.* evil-doer.

Fangled, *adj.* fond of novelties.

Fap, *adj.* drunk.

Farced, *p.p.* stuffed out.

Fardel, *sb.* a burden, bundle.

Fat, *adj.* cloying. *sb.* vat.

Favour, *sb.* outward appearance, aspect. In pl. = features.

Fear, *v.t.* to frighten. 3 H VI. III. 3. 226. Fear for. M. of V. III. 5. 3.

Feat, *adj.* neat, dexterous.

Feat, *v.t.* to fashion, form.

Fee, *sb.* worth, value.

Feeder, *sb.* servant.

Fee-farm, *sb.* a tenure without limit of time.

Fellowly, *adj.* companionable, sympathetic.

Feodary, *sb.* confederate.

Fere, *sb.* spouse, consort.

Ferret, *v.t.* to worry.

Festinate, *adj.* swift, speedy.

Fet, *p.p.* fetched.

Fico, *sb.* a fig (Span.).

File, *sb.* list.

File, *v.t.* to defile. Mac. III. 1. 65. Smooth, polish. L.L.L. V.
   1. 11. *v.i.* to walk in file. H VIII. III. 2. 171.

Fill-horse, *sb.* a shaft-horse.

Fills, *sb.* shafts.

Fineless, *adj.* endless, infinite.

Firago, *sb.* virago.

Firk, *v.t.* to beat.

Fitchew, *sb.* pole-cat.

Fitment, *sb.* that which befits.

Flap-dragon, *sb.* snap-dragon, or small burning object,
   lighted and floated in a glass of liquor, to be swallowed
   burning. L.L.L. V. 1. 43. 2 H IV. II. 4. 244. *v.t.* to swallow
   like a flap-dragon. W.T. III. 3.100.

Flaw, *sb.* gust of wind. Ham. V. 1. 223. Small flake of ice. 2
   H IV. IV. 4. 35. Passionate outburst. M. for M. II. 3. 11. A
   crack. Lear, II. 4. 288. *v.t.* make a flaw in, break. H VIII.
   I. 1. 95; I. 2. 21.

Fleer, *sb.* sneer. Oth. IV. 1. 83. *v.i.* to grin; sneer. L.L.L. V.
   2. 109.

Fleshment, *sb.* encouragement given by first success.

Flewed, *p.p.* with large hanging chaps.

Flight, *sb.* a long light arrow.

Flighty, *adj.* swift.

Flirt-gill, *sb.* light wench.

Flote, *sb.* sea.

Flourish, *v.t.* to ornament, gloss over.

Fobbed, *p.p.* cheated, deceived.

Foil, *sb.* defeat. 1 H VI. III. 3. 11. *v.t.* to defeat, mar. Pass.
   P. 99

Foin, *v.i.* to thrust (in fencing).

Fopped, *p.p.* cheated, fooled.

Forbod, *p.p.* forbidden.

Fordo, *v.t.* to undo, destroy.

Foreign, *adj.* dwelling abroad.

Fork, *sb.* the forked tongue of a snake. M. for M. III. 1. 16. The barbed head of an arrow. Lear, I. 1. 146. The junction of the legs with the trunk. Lear. IV. 6. 120.

Forked, *p.p.* barbed. As II. 1. 24. Horned as a cuckold. T. & C. I. 2. 164.

Forslow, *v.i.* to delay.

Forspeak, *v.t.* to speak against.

Fosset-seller, *sb.* a seller of taps.

Fox, *sb.* broadsword.

Foxship, *sb.* selfish and ungrateful, cunning.

Fracted, *p.p.* broken.

Frampold, *adj.* turbulent, quarrelsome.

Frank, *v.t.* to pen in a frank or sty. R III. 1. 3. 314. *sb.* a sty. 2 H IV. II. 2. 145. *adj.* liberal. Lear, III. 4. 20.

Franklin, *sb.* a yeoman.

Fraught, *sb.* freight, cargo, load. Tw.N. V. 1. 59. *v.t.* to load, burden. Cym. I. 1. 126. *p.p.* laden. M. of V. II. 8. 30. Stored. Two G. III. 2. 70.

Fraughtage, *sb.* cargo. C. of E. IV. 1. 8.

Fraughting, *part. adj.* constituting the cargo.

Frize, *sb.* a kind of coarse woollen cloth with a nap.

Frontier, *sb.* an outwork in fortification. 1 H IV. II. 3. 56. Used figuratively. 1 H IV. I. 3. 19.

Fruitful, *adj.* bountiful, plentiful.

Frush, *v.t.* to bruise, batter.

Frutify, blunder for certify. M. of V II. 2. 132.

Fubbed off, *p.p.* put off with excuses. 2 H IV. II. 1. 34.

Fullams, *sb.* a kind of false dice.

Gad, *sb.* a pointed instrument. T.A. IV. 1. 104. Upon the gad = on the spur of the moment, hastily. Lear, I. 2. 26.

Gage, *v.t.* to pledge.

Gaingiving, *sb.* misgiving.

Galliard, *sb.* a lively dance.

Gallimaufry, *sb.* medley, tumble.

Gallow, *v.t.* to frighten.

Gallowglass, *sb.* heavy- armed Irish foot-soldier.

Gallows, *sb.* a rogue, one fit to be hung.

Gallows-bird, *sb.* one that merits hanging.

Garboil, *sb.* uproar, commotion.

Gaskins, *sb.* loose breeches.

Gastness, *sb.* ghastliness, terror.

Geck, *sb.* dupe.

Generation, *sb.* offspring.

Generous, *adj.* nobly born.

Gennet, *sb.* a Spanish horse.

Gentry, *sb.* rank by birth. M.W. W. II. 1. 51. Courtesy. Ham. II. 2. 22.

German, *sb.* a near kinsman.

Germen, *sb.* germ, seed.

Gest, *sb.* a period of sojourn; originally the halting place in a royal progress.

Gib, *sb.* an old rom-cat.

Gibbet, *v.t.* to hang, as a barrel when it is slung.

Gig, *sb.* top.

Giglot, *adj.* wanton. 1 H VI. IV. 7. 41. *sb.* M. for M. V. 1. 345.

Gillyvors, *sb.* gillyflowers.

Gimmal-bit, *sb.* a double bit, or one made with double rings.

Gimmer, *sb.* contrivance, mechanical device.

Ging, *sb.* gang, pack.

Gird, *sb.* a scoff, jest. 2 H VI. III. 1. 131. *v.t.* to taunt, gibe at. 2 H IV. I. 2. 6.

Gleek, *sb.* scoff. 1 H VI. IV. 2. 12. *v.i.* to scoff. M.N.D. III. 1. 145.

Glib, *v.t.* to geld.

Gloze, *v.i.* to comment. H V. I. 2. 40. T. & C. II. 2. 165. To use flattery. R II. II. 1. 10; T.A. IV. 4. 35.

Gnarling, *pr.p.* snarling.

Godden, *sb.* good den, good even.

God'ild, God yield, God reward.

God-jer = good-year.

Good-year, *sb.* a meaningless interjection. M.A. I. 3. I. Some malific power. Lear, V. 3. 24.

Goss, *sb.* gorse.

Gossip, *sb.* sponsor. Two G. III. 1. 269. *v.t.* to stand sponsor for. A. W. I. 1. 176.

Gorbellied, *adj.* big-bellied.

Graff, *sb.* graft, scion. *v.t.* to graft.

Grain, *sb.* a fast colour. Hence in grain = ingrained.

Gratillity, *sb.* gratuity.

Gratulate, *adj.* gratifying.

Greek, *sb.* boon companion.

Grise, *sb.* a step.

Guard, *v.t.* to trim, ornament.

Guardant, *sb.* sentinel, guard.

Guidon, *sb.* standard, banner.

Gules, *adj.* red, in heraldry.

Gust, *sb.* taste. *v.t.* to taste.

Hackney, *sb.* loose woman.

Haggard, *sb.* untrained hawk.

Haggled, *p.p.* hacked, mangled.

Hair, *sb.* texture, nature. I H IV. IV. 1. 61. Against the hair = against the grain. R. & J. II. 3. 97.

Handfast, *sb.* betrothal, contract. Cym. I. 5. 78. Custody. W.T. IV. 3. 778.

Handsaw, *sb.* corruption of heronshaw, a heron.

Hardiment, *sb.* daring deed.

Harlot, *adj.* lewd, base.

Hatched, *p.p.* closed with a hatch or half door. Per. IV. 2. 33. Engraved. T. & C. I. 3. 65.

Havoc, to cry havoc = cry no quarter. John, II. 1. 357. *v.t.* cut to pieces, destroy. H V. I. 2. 193.

Hawking, *adj.* hawk-like.

Hay, *sb.* a round dance. L.L.L. V. 1. 147. A term in fencing when a hit is made (Ital. *hai*, you have it). R. & J. II. 4. 27.

Hebenon, *sb.* perhaps the yew (Germ. *Eiben*). Ebony and henbane have been suggested.

Hefts, *sb.* heavings.

Helm, *v.t.* to steer.

Helpless, *adj.* not helping, useless. R III. I. 2. 13; Lucr. 1027. Incurable, Lucr. 756.

Hent, *sb.* grasp, hold. Ham. III. 3. 88. *v.t.* to hold, pass. M. for M. IV. 6. 14.

Hermit, *sb.* beadsman, one bound to pray for another.

Hild = held.

Hilding, *sb.* a good-for-nothing.

Hoar, *adj.* mouldy, R. & J. II. 3. 136. *v.i.* to become mouldy. R. & J. II. 3. 142.

Hoar, *v.t.* to make hoary or white, as with leprosy.

Hobby-horse, *sb.* a principal figure in the old morris dance. L.L.L. III. 1. 30. A light woman. M.A. III. 2. 68.

Hob-nob, have or not have, hit or miss.

Hold in, *v.i.* to keep counsel.

Holding, *sb.* the burden of a song. A. & C. II. 7. 112. Fitness, sense. A.W. IV. 2. 27.

Holy-ales, *sb.* rural festivals.

Honest, *adj.* chaste.

Honesty, *sb.* chastity. M.W.W. II. 2. 234. Decency. Tw.N. II. 3. 85. Generosity, liberality. Tim. III. 1. 30.

Honey-seed, blunder for homicide, 2 H IV. II. 1. 52.

Honey-suckle, blunder for homicidal. 2 H IV. II. 1. 50.

Hoodman, *sb.* the person blinded in the game of hoodman-blind.

Hoodman-blind, *sb.* blind-man's buff.

Hot at hand, not to be held in.

Hot-house, *sb.* bagnio, often in fact a brothel as well.

Hox, *v.t.* to hough, hamstring.

Hoy, *sb.* a small coasting vessel.

Hugger-mugger, In, stealthily and secretly.

Hull, *v.i.* to float.

Hulling, *pr. p.* floating at the mercy of the waves.

Ignomy, *sb.* ignominy.

Imbar, *v.t.* to bar in, make secure. H V. I. 2. 94.

Imboss, *v.t.* to hunt to death.

Imbossed, *p.p.* swollen. As II. 7. 67. Foaming at the mouth. T. of S. Ind. I. 16.

Immanity, *sb.* savageness, ferocity.

Immoment, *adj.* insignificant.

Immures, *sb.* surrounding walls.

Imp, *v.t.* to graft new feathers to a falcon's wing.

Impair, *adj.* unsuitable.

Impale, *v.t.* to encircle.

Impart, *v.t.* to afford, grant. Lucr. 1039; Sonn. LXXII. 8. *v.i.* to behave oneself. Ham. I. 2. 112.

Imperceiverant, *adj.* lacking in perception.

Impeticos, *v.t.* to put in the petticoat or pocket.

Importance, *sb.* importunity. John, II. 1. 7. Import. W.T. V. 2. 19. Question at issue, that which is imported. Cym. I. 5. 40.

Imposition, *sb.* command, injunction. M. of V. I. 2. 106. Penalty. M. for M. I. 2. 186.

Imposthume, *sb.* abscess.

Imprese, *sb.* device with a motto.

Include, *v.t.* to conclude, end.

Incontinent, *adj.* immediate.

Incony, *adj.* dainty, delicate.

Indent, *v.i.* to make terms.

Index, *sb.* introduction (in old books the index came first).

Indifferency, *sb.* impartiality.

Indirectly, *adv.* wrongly, unjustly.

Indurance, *sb.* durance, imprisonment.

Infest, *v.t.* to vex, trouble.

Inherit, *v.t.* to possess. Tp. IV. 1. 154. To cause to possess, put in possession. R II. I. 1. 85. *v.i.* to take possession. Tp. II. 2. 182.

Inheritor, *sb.* possessor.

Injury, *sb.* insult.

Inkhorn mate, *sb.* bookworm.

Inkle, *sb.* coarse tape.

Insisture, *sb.* persistence.

Intenible, *adj.* incapable of holding.

Intention, *sb.* aim, direction.

Intermissive, *adj.* intermitted, interrupted.

Intrinse, *adj.* tightly drawn.

Invised, *adj.* unseen, a doubtful word.

Irregulous, *adj.* lawless.

Jack, *sb.* figure that struck the bell in old clocks. R III. IV. 2. 114.
A term of contempt. R III. I. 3. 72. The small bowl aimed at
in the game of bowls. Cym. II. 1. 2. The key of a virginal.
Sonn. CXXVIII. 5. A drinking vessel. T. of S. IV. 1. 48.

Jade, *v.t.* to play the jade with, run away with. Tw.N. II. 5.
164. Drive like a jade. A. & C. III. 1. 34. Treat with
contempt. H VIII. III. 2. 280.

Jakes, *sb.* a privy.

Jar, *sb.* a tick of the clock. W.T. I. 2. 43.

Jar, *v.t.* to tick. R II. V. 5. 51. *v.i.* to guard. I H VI. III. 1. 70.
sb. a quarrel. I H VI. I. 1. 44.

Jesses, *sb.* straps attaching the legs of a hawk to the fist.

Jet, *v.i.* to strut. Tw.N. II. 4. 32. Advance threateningly. R
III. II. 4. 51.

Journal, *adj.* diurnal, daily.

Jowl, *v.t.* to knock, dash.

Kam, *adj.* crooked, away from the point.

Keech, *sb.* a lump of tallow or fat.

Keel, *v.t.* to cool.

Ken, *sb.* perception, sight. *v.t.* to know.

Kern, *sb.* light-armed foot-soldier of Ireland.

Kibe, *sb.* chilblain on the heel.

Kicky-wicky, *sb.* a pet name.

Killen = to kill.

Kiln-hole, *sb.* the fireplace of an oven or kiln.

Kind, *sb.* nature. M. of V. I. 3. 84. *adj.* natural. Lucr. 1423. *adv.* kindly. Tim. I. 2. 224.

Kindle, *v.t.* to bring forth young. As III. 2. 343. Incite. As I. 1. 179.

Knack, *sb.* a pretty trifle.

Knap, *v.t.* to gnaw, nibble. M. of V. III. 1. 9. Rap. Lear, II. 4. 123.

Laboursome, *adj.* elaborate.

Laced mutton, *sb.* slang for courtesan.

Lade, *v.t.* to empty, drain.

Land-damn. Unrecognizably corrupt word in W.T. II. 1. 143.

Lapsed, *p.p.* caught, surprised. Tw.N. III. 3. 36.

Latch, *v.t.* to catch, lay hold of.

Latten, *sb.* a mixture of copper and tin. M.W.W. I. 1. 153.

Laund, *sb.* glade.

Lavolt, *sb.* a dance in which two persons bound high and whirl round.

Lay for, *v.t.* to strive to win.

Leasing, *sb.* lying, falsehood.

Leave, *sb.* liberty, license.

Leer, *sb.* complexion.

Leese, *v.t.* to lose.

Leet, *sb.* a manor court. T. of S. Ind. II. 87. The time when such is held. Oth. III. 3. 140.

Leiger, *sb.* ambassador.

Length, *sb.* delay.

Let, *v.t.* to hinder. Tw.N. V. 1. 246; Ham. I. 4. 85. Detain. W.T. I. 2. 41. Forbear. Lucr. 10. *p.p.* caused. Ham. IV. 6. 11. *sb.* hindrance. H V. V. 2. 65.

Let-alone, *sb.* hindrance, prohibition.

Level, *sb.* aim, line of fire. R. & J. III. 3. 102. *v.i.* to aim. R III. IV. 4. 202. Be on the same level. Oth. I. 3. 239. *adv.* evenly. Tw.N. II. 4. 32.

Lewd, *adj.* base, vile.

Libbard, *sb.* leopard.

Liberal, *adj.* licentious. Liberal conceit = elaborate design. Ham. V. 2. 152. *adv.* freely, openly. Oth. V. 2. 220.

Lieger, *sb.* ambassador.

Lifter, *sb.* thief.

Light, *p.p.* lighted.

Likelihood, *sb.* sign, indication.

Lime, *v.t.* to put lime into liquor. M.W.W. I. 3. 14. Smear with bird-lime. 2 H VI. I. 3. 86. Catch with bird-lime. Tw.N. III. 4. 75. Cement. 3 H VI. V. 1. 84.

Limit, *sb.* appointed time. R II. I. 3. 151. *v.t.* to appoint. John. V. 2. 123.

Line, *v.t.* to draw, paint. As III. 2. 93. Strengthen, fortify. I H IV. II. 3. 85.

Line-grove, *sb.* a grove of lime trees.

Linsey-woolsey, *sb.* gibberish (literally, mixed stuff).

Lipsbury pinfold. Perhaps = between the teeth.

List, *sb.* desire, inclination. Oth. II. 1. 105. Limit, boundary. I H IV. IV. 1. 51. Lists for combat. Mac. III. 1. 70.

Lither, *adj.* flexible, gentle.

Livery, *sb.* delivery of a freehold into the possession of the heir.

Lob, *sb.* lubber, lout.

Lockram, *sb.* coarse linen.

Lodge, *v.t.* to lay flat, beat down.

Loggats, *sb.* a game somewhat resembling bowls.

Loof, *v.t.* to luff, bring close to the wind.

Losel, *sb.* a wasteful, worthless fellow.

Lout, *v.t.* to make a lout or fool of.

Lown, *sb.* base fellow.

Luce, *sb.* pike or jack.

Lurch, *v.t.* to win a love set at a game; bear off the prize easily. Cor. II. 2. 102. *v.i.* to skulk. M. W. W. II. 2. 25.

Lym, *sb.* bloodhound; so called from the leam or leash used to hold him.

Maggot-pie, *sb.* magpie.

Main, *sb.* a call at dice. I H IV. IV. 1. 47. Mainland. Lear, III. 1. 6. The chief power. Ham. V. 4. 15.

Main-course, *sb.* mainsail.

Main'd, *p.p.* maimed.

Makeless, *adj.* mateless, widowed.

Malkin, *sb.* slattern.

Mallard, *sb.* a wild drake.

Mallecho, *sb.* mischief (Span. *malhecho*).

Malt-horse, *sb.* brewer's horse.

Mammering, *pr.p.* hesitating.

Mammet, *sb.* a doll.

Mammock, *v.t.* to tear in pieces.

Manakin, *sb.* little man.

Mankind, *adj.* masculine, applied to a woman.

Manner, with the = in the act, red-handed.

Mare, *sb.* nightmare. To ride the wild mare = play at see-saw.

Mark, *sb.* thirteen shillings and fourpence.

Mart, *v.i.* to market, traffic. Cym. I. 6. 150. *v.t.* to vend, traffic with. J. C. IV. 3. 11.

Mastic, *sb.* used to stop decayed teeth.

Match, *sb.* compact, bargain. M. of V. III. 1. 40. Set a match = make an appointment. 1 H IV. 1. 2. 110.

Mate, *v.t.* to confound, make bewildered. C. of E. III. 2. 54. Match, cope with. H VIII. III. 2. 274.

Material, *adj.* full of matter.

Maugre, *prep.* in spite of.

Maund, *sb.* a basket.

Mazard, *sb.* skull.

Meacock, *adj.* spiritless, pusillanimous.

Mealed. *p.p.* mingled, compounded.

Mean, *sb.* the intermediate part between the tenor and treble.

Meiny, *sb.* attendants, retinue.

Mell, *v.i.* to meddle.

Mered, He being the mered question—the question concerning him alone. A. & C. III. 13. 10.

Mess, *sb,* a set of four. L.L.L. IV. 3. 204. Small quantity. 2 H IV. II. 1. 95. Lower messes = inferiors, as messing at the lower end of the table. W.T. I. 2. 226.

Mete, *v. i.* to mete at = aim at.

Metheglin, *sb.* a kind of mead, made of honey and water.

Micher, *sb.* truant.

Miching, *adj.* sneaking, stealthy.

Mineral, *sb.* a mine.

Minikin, *adj.* small, pretty.

Minion, *sb.* darling, favourite. John, II. 1. 392. Used contemptuously. 2 H VI. I. 3. 82. A pert, saucy person. 2 H VI. I. 3. 136.

Mirable, *adj.* admirable.

Mire, *v.i.* to be bemired, sink as into mire.

Misdread, *sb.* fear of evil.

Misprision, *sb.* mistake. M.N.D. III. 2. 90. Contempt. A.W. II. 3. 153.

Misproud, *adj.* viciously proud.

Miss, *sb.* misdoing.

Missingly, *adv.* regretfully.

Missive, *sb.* messenger.

Misthink, *v.t.* to misjudge.

Mobled, *p.p.* having the face or head muffled.

Modern, *adj.* commonplace, trite.

Module, *sb.* mould, form.

Moldwarp, *sb.* mole.

Mome, *sb.* blockhead, dolt.

Momentany, *adj.* momentary, lasting an instant.

Monster, *v.t.* to make monstrous.

Month's mind, *sb.* intense desire or yearning.

Moralize, *v.t.* to interpret, explain.

Mort, *sb.* trumpet notes blown at the death of the deer.

Mortal, *adj.* deadly.

Mortified, *p.p.* deadened, insensible.

Mot, *sb.* motto, device.

Mother, *sb.* the disease *hysterica passio.*

Motion, *v.t.* to propose, counsel. 1 H VI. I. 3. 63. *sb.* a puppet show. W.T. IV. 3. 96. A puppet. Two G. II. 1. 91. Solicitation, proposal, suit. C. of E. I. 1. 60. Emotion, feeling, impulse. Tw.N. II. 4. 18.

Motive, *sb.* a mover, instrument, member.

Mountant, *adj.* lifted up.

Mow, *sb.* a grimace. *v.i.* to grimace.

Moy, *sb.* probably some coin.

Muleter, *sb. muleteer.*

Mulled, *p.p.* flat, insipid.

Mummy, *sb.* a medical or magical preparation originally made from mummies.

Murdering-piece, *sb.* a cannon loaded with chain-shot.

Murrion, *adj.* infected with the murrain.

Muse, *v.i.* to wonder. John, III. 1. 317. *v.t.* to wonder at. Tp. III. 3. 36.

Muset, *sb.* a gap or opening in a hedge.

Muss, *sb.* scramble.

Mutine, *sb.* mutineer.

Mystery, *sb.* profession. M. for M. IV. 2. 28. Professional skill. A.W. III. 6. 65.

Nayword, *sb.* pass-word, M.W.W. II. 2. 126. A by-word. Tw.N. II. 3. 132.

Neat, *adj.* trim, spruce.

Neb, *sb.* bill or beak.

Neeld, *sb.* needle.

Neeze, *v.i.* to sneeze.

Neif, *sb.* fist.

Next, *adj.* nearest.

Nick, *sb.* out of all nick, beyond all reckoning.

Night-rule, *sb.* revelry.

Nill = will not.

Nine-men's-morris, *sb.* a rustic game.

Note, *sb.* list, catalogue. W.T. IV. 2. 47. Note of expectation = list of expected guests. Mac. III. 3. 10. Stigma, mark of reproach. R II. 1. 1. 43. Distinction. Cym. II. 3. 12. knowledge, observation. Lear, III. 1. 18.

Nott-pated, *adj.* crop-headed.

Nousle, *v.t.* to nurse, nourish delicately.

Nowl, *sb.* noddle.

Nuthook, *sb.* slang for catchpole.

Oathable, *adj.* capable of taking an oath.

Object, *sb.* anything presented to the sight; everything that comes in the way.

Obsequious, *adj.* regardful of funeral rites. 3 H VI. II. 5. 118. Funereal, having to do with obsequies. T. A. V. 3. 153.

Observance, *sb.* observation. Oth. III. 3. 151. Homage. 2 H IV. IV. 3. 15. Ceremony. M. of V. II. 2. 194.

Obstacle, *sb.* blunder for obstinate.

Occupation, *sb.* trade (in contemptuous sense). Cor. IV. 1. 14. Voice of occupation = vote of working men. Cor. IV. 6. 98.

Odd, *adj.* unnoticed. Tp. I. 2. 223. At odds. T. & C. IV. 5. 265.

Oeillades, *sb.* amorous glances.

O' ergrown, *p.p.* bearded. Cym. IV. 4. 33. Become too old. M. for M. I. 3. 22.

O'erstrawed, *p.p.* overstrewn.

Office, *v.t.* to office all = do all the domestic service. A. W. III. 2. 128. Keep officiously. Cor. V. 2. 61.

Oneyers, *sb.* unexplained word.

Opposition, *sb.* combat, encounter.

Orb, *sb.* orbit. R. & J. II. 1. 151. Circle. M.N.D. II. 1. 9. A heavenly body. M. of V. V. 1. 60. The earth. Tw.N. III. 1. 39.

Ordinant, *adj.* ordaining, controlling.

Ordinary, *sb.* a public dinner at which each man pays for his own share.

Ort, *sb.* remnant, refuse.

Ouphs, *sb.* elves, goblins.

Outrage, *sb.* outburst of rage.

Overscutch'd, *p.p.* over-whipped, over-switched (perhaps in a wanton sense).

Overture, *sb.* disclosure. W.T. II. 1. 172. Declaration. Tw.N. I. 5. 208.

Owe, *v.t.* to own, possess.

Packing, *sb.* plotting, conspiracy.

Paddock, *sb.* toad. Ham. III. 4. 191. A familiar spirit in the form of a toad. Mac. I. 1. 9.

Pajock, *sb.* term of contempt, by some said to mean peacock.

Pale, *sb.* enclosure, confine.

Palliament, *sb.* robe.

Parcel-bawd, *sb.* half-bawd.

Paritor, *sb.* apparitor, an officer of the Bishops' Court.

Part, *sb.* party, side.

Partake, *v.t.* to make to partake, impart. W.T. V. 3. 132. To share. J.C. II. 1. 305.

Parted, *p.p.* endowed.

Partisan, *sb.* a kind of pike.

Pash, *sb.* a grotesque word for the head. W.T. I. 2. 128. *v.t.* to smite, dash. T. & C. II. 3. 202.

Pass, *v.t.* to pass sentence on. M. for M. II. 1. 19. Care for. 2 H VI. IV. 2. 127. Represent. L.L.L. V. 1. 123. Make a thrust in fencing. Tw.N. III. 1. 44.

Passage, *sb.* passing to and fro. C. of E. III. 1. 99. Departure, death. Ham. III. 3. 86. Passing away. 1 H VI. II. 5. 108. Occurrence. A.W. I. 1. 19. Process, course. R. & J. Prol. 9. Thy passages of life = the actions of thy life. 1 H IV. III. 2. 8. Passages of grossness = gross impositions. Tw.N. III. 2. 70. Motion. Cor. V. 6. 76.

Passant. In heraldry, the position of an animal walking.

Passion, *sb.* passionate poem. M.N.D. V. 1. 306; Sonn. XX. 2.

Passionate, *v.t.* to express with emotion. T.A. III. 2. 6. *adj.* displaying emotion. 2 H VI. I. 1. 104. Sorrowful. John, II. 1. 544.

Passy measures, a corruption of the Italian *passamezzo*, denoting a stately and measured step in dancing.

Patch, *sb.* fool.

Patchery, *sb.* knavery, trickery.

Patronage, *v.t.* to patronize, protect.

Pavin, *sb.* a stately dance of Spanish or Italian origin.

Pawn, *sb.* a pledge.

Peach, *v.t.* to impeach, accuse.

Peat, *sb.* pet, darling.

Pedascule, *sb.* vocative, pedant, schoolmaster.

Peevish, *adj.* childish, silly. 1 H VI. V. 3. 186. Fretful, wayward. M. of V. I. 1. 86.

Peise, *v.t.* to poise, balance. John, II. 1. 575. Retard by making heavy. M. of V. III. 2. 22. Weigh down. R III. V. 3. 106.

Pelt, *v.i.* to let fly with words of opprobrium.

Pelting, *adj.* paltry.

Penitent, *adj.* doing penance.

Periapt, *sb.* amulet.

Period, *sb.* end, conclusion. A. & C. IV. 2. 25. *v.t.* to put an end to. Tim. I. 1. 103.

Perked up, *p.p.* dressed up.

Perspective, *sb.* glasses so fashioned as to create an optical illusion.

Pert, *adj.* lively, brisk.

Pertaunt-like, *adv.* word unexplained and not yet satisfactorily amended. L.L.L. V. 2. 67.

Pervert, *v.t.* to avert, turn aside.

Pettitoes, *sb.* feet; properly pig's feet.

Pheeze, *v.t.* beat, chastise, torment.

Phisnomy, *sb.* physiognomy.

Phraseless, *adj.* indescribable.

Physical, *adj.* salutary, wholesome.

Pia mater, *sb.* membrane that covers the brain; used for the brain itself.

Pick, *v.t.* to pitch, throw.

Picked, *p.p.* refined, precise.

Picking, *adj.* trifling, small.

Piece, *sb.* a vessel of wine.

Pight, *p.p.* pitched.

Piled, *p.p* = peeled, bald, with quibble on 'piled' of velvet.

Pill, *v.t.* to pillage, plunder.

Pin, *sb*. bull's-eye of a target.

Pin-buttock, *sb*. a narrow buttock.

Pioned, *adj*. doubtful word: perhaps covered with marsh-marigold, or simply dug.

Pip, *sb*. a spot on cards. A pip out = intoxicated, with reference to a game called one and thirty.

Pitch, *sb*. the height to which a falcon soars, height.

Placket, *sb*. opening in a petticoat, or a petticoat.

Planched, *adj*. made of planks.

Plantage, *sb*. plants, vegetation.

Plantation, *sb*. colonizing.

Plausive, *adj*. persuasive, pleasing.

Pleached, *adj*. interlaced, folded.

Plurisy, *sb*. superabundance.

Point-devise, *adj*. precise, finical. L.L.L. V. 1.19. *adv*. Tw.N. II. 5. 162.

Poking-sticks, *sb*. irons for setting out ruffs.

Pole-clipt, *adj*. used of vineyards in which the vines are grown around poles.

Polled, *adj*. clipped, laid bare.

Pomander, *sb*. a ball of perfume.

Poor-John, *sb*. salted and dried hake.

Porpentine, *sb*. porcupine.

Portable, *adj*. supportable, endurable.

Portage, *sb*. port-hole. H V. III. 1. 10. Port-dues. Per. III. 1. 35.

Portance, *sb*. deportment, bearing.

Posse, *v.t*. to curdle.

Posy, *sb*. a motto on a ring.

Potch, *v.i*. to poke, thrust.

Pottle, *sb*. a tankard; strictly a two quart measure.

Pouncet-box, *sb*. a box for perfumes, pierced with holes.

Practice, *sb*. plot.

Practisant, *sb*. accomplice.

Practise, *v.i*. to plot, use stratagems. Two G. IV. 1. 47. *v.t*. to plot. John, IV. 1. 20.

Precedent, *sb*. rough draft. R III. III. 6. 7. Prognostic, indication. V. & A. 26.

Prefer, *v.t.* to promote, advance. Two G. II. 4. 154. Recommend. Cym. II. 3. 50. Present offer. M.N.D. IV. 2. 37.

Pregnant, *adj.* ready-witted, clever. Tw.N. II. 2. 28. Full of meaning. Ham. II. 2. 209. Ready. Ham. III. 2. 66. Plain, evident. M. for M. II. 1. 23.

Prenzie, *adj.* demure.

Pretence, *sb.* project, scheme.

Prick, *sb.* point on a dial. 3 H VI. I. 4. 34. Bull's-eye. L.L.L. IV. I. 132. Prickle. As III. 2. 113. Skewer. Lear, II. 3. 16.

Pricket, *sb.* a buck of the second year.

Prick-song, *sb.* music sung from notes.

Prig, *sb.* a thief.

Private, *sb.* privacy. Tw.N. III. 4. 90. Private communication. John, IV. 3. 16.

Prize, *sb.* prize-contest. T.A. I. 1. 399. Privilege. 3 H VI. I. 4. 59. Value. Cym. III. 6. 76.

Probal, *adj.* probable, reasonable.

Proditor, *sb.* traitor.

Proface, *int.* much good may it do you!

Propagate, *v.t.* to augment.

Propagation, *sb.* augmentation.

Proper-false, *adj.* handsome and deceitful.

Property, *sb.* a tool or instrument. M.W.W. III. 4. 10. *v.t.* to make a tool of. John, V. 2. 79.

Pugging, *adj.* thievish.

Puisny, *adj.* unskilful, like a tyro.

Pun, *v.t.* to pound.

Punk, *sb.* strumpet.

Purchase, *v.t.* to acquire, get. *sb.* acquisition, booty.

Pursuivant, *sb.* a herald's attendant or messenger.

Pursy, *adj.* short-winded, asthmatic.

Puttock, *sb.* a kite.

Puzzel, *sb.* a filthy drab (Italian *puzzolente*).

Quaintly, *adv.* ingeniously, deliberately.

Qualification, *sb.* appeasement.

Quality, *sb.* profession, calling, especially that of an actor. Two G. IV. 1. 58. Professional skill. Tp. I. 2. 193.

Quarter, *sb.* station. John, V. 5. 20. Keep fair quarter = keep on good terms with, be true to. C. of E. II. 1. 108. In quarter = on good terms. Oth. II. 3. 176.

Quat, *sb.* pimple.

Quatch-buttock, *sb.* a squat or flat buttock.

Quean, *sb.* wench, hussy.

Queasiness, *sb.* nausea, disgust.

Queasy, *adj.* squeamish, fastidious. M.A. II. 1. 368. Disgusted. A. & C. III. 6. 20.

Quell, *sb.* murder.

Quest, *sb.* inquest, jury. R III. I. 4. 177. Search, inquiry, pursuit. M. of V. I. 1. 172. A body of searchers. Oth. I. 2. 46.

Questant, *sb.* aspirant, candidate.

Quicken, *v.t.* to make alive. A.W. II. 1. 76. Refresh, revive. M. of V. II. 7. 52. *v.i.* to become alive, revive. Lear, III. 7. 40.

Quietus, *sb.* settlement of an account.

Quill, *sb.* body. 2 H VI. I. 3. 3.

Quillet, *sb.* quibble.

Quintain, *sb.* a figure set up for tilting at.

Quire, *sb.* company.

Quittance, *v.i.* to requite. 1 H VI. II. 1. 14. *sb.* acquittance. M. W. W. I. 1. 10. Requital. 2 H IV. I. 1. 108.

Quoif, *sb.* cap.

Quoit, *v.t.* to throw.

Quote, *v.t.* to note, examine.

Rabato, *sb.* a kind of ruff.

Rabbit-sucker, *sb.* sucking rabbit.

Race, *sb.* root. W.T. IV. 3. 48. Nature, disposition. M. for M. II. 4. 160. Breed. Mac. II. 4. 15.

Rack, *v.t.* stretch, strain. M. of V. I. 1. 181. Strain to the utmost. *Cor.* V. 1. 16.

Rack, *sb.* a cloud or mass of clouds. Ham. II. 2. 492. *v.i.* move like vapour. 3 H VI. II. 1. 27.

Rampired, *p.p.* fortified by a rampart.

Ramps, *sb.* wanton wenches.

Ranges, *sb.* ranks.

Rap, *v.t.* to transport.

Rascal, *sb.* a deer out of condition.

Raught, *impf.* & *p.p.* reached.

Rayed, *p.p.* befouled. T. of S. IV. 1. 3. In T. of S. III. 2. 52 it perhaps means arrayed, *i.e.* attacked.

Raze, *sb.* root.

Razed, *p.p.* slashed.

Reave, *v.t.* to bereave.

Rebate, *v.t.* to make dull, blunt.

Recheat, *sb.* a set of notes sounded to call hounds off a false scent.

Rede, *sb.* counsel.

Reechy, *adj.* smoky, grimy.

Refell, *v.t.* to refute.

Refuse, *sb.* rejection, disowning. *v.t.* to reject, disown.

Reguerdon, *v.t.* to reward, guerdon.

Remonstrance, *sb.* demonstration.

Remotion, *sb.* removal.

Renege, *v.t.* to deny.

Renying, *pres. p.* denying.

Replication, *sb.* echo. J.C. I. 1. 50. Reply. Ham. IV. 2. 12.

Rere-mice, *sb.* bats.

Respected, blunder for suspected.

Respective, *adj.* worthy of regard. Two G. IV. 4. 197. Showing regard. John, I. 1. 188. Careful. M. of V. V. 1. 156.

Respectively, *adv.* respectfully.

Rest, *sb.* set up one's rest is to stand upon the cards in one's hand, be fully resolved.

Resty, *adj.* idle, lazy.

Resume, *v.t.* to take.

Reverb, *v.t.* to resound.

Revolt, *sb.* rebel.

Ribaudred, *adj.* ribald, lewd.

Rid, *v.t.* to destroy, do away with.

Riggish, *adj.* wanton.

Rigol, *sb.* a circle.

Rim, *sb.* midriff or abdomen.

Rivage, *sb.* shore.

Rival, *sb.* partner, companion. M.N.D. III. 2. 156. *v.i.* to be a competitor. Lear, I. 1. 191.

Rivality, *sb.* partnership, participation.

Rivelled, *adj.* wrinkled.

Road, *sb.* roadstead, port. Two G. II. 4. 185. Journey. H VIII. IV. 2. 17. Inroad, incursion. H V. I. 2. 138.

Roisting, *adj.* roistering, blustering.

Romage, *sb.* bustle, turmoil.

Ronyon, *sb.* scurvy wretch.

Rook, *v.i.* to cower, squat.

Ropery, *sb.* roguery.

Rope-tricks, *sb.* knavish tricks.

Roping, *pr.p.* dripping.

Roted, *p.p.* learned by heart.

Rother, *sb.* an ox, or animal of the ox kind.

Round, *v.i.* to whisper. John, II. 1. 566. *v.t.* to surround. M.N.D. IV. 1. 52.

Round, *adj.* straightforward, blunt, plainspoken. C. of E. II. 1. 82.

Rouse, *sb.* deep draught, bumper.

Rout, *sb.* crowd, mob. C. of E. III. 1. 101. Brawl. Oth. II. 3. 210.

Row, *sb.* verse or stanza.

Roynish, *adj.* scurvy; hence coarse, rough.

Rub, *v.i.* to encounter obstacles. L.L.L. IV. 1. 139. Rub on, of a bowl that surmounts the obstacle in its course. T. & C. III. 2. 49. *sb.* impediment, hindrance; from the game of bowls. John, III. 4. 128.

Ruffle, *v.i.* to swagger, bully. T.A. I. 1. 314.

Ruddock, *sb.* the redbreast.

Rudesby, *sb.* a rude fellow.

Rump-fed, *adj.* pampered; perhaps fed on offal, or else fat-rumped.

Running banquet, a hasty refreshment (fig.).

Rush aside, *v.t.* to pass hasitily by, thrust aside.

Rushling, blunder for rustling.

Sad, *adj.* grave, serious. M. of V. II. 2. 195. Gloomy, sullen. R II. V. 5. 70.

Sagittary, *sb.* a centaur. T. & C. V. 5. 14. The official residence in the arsenal at Venice. Oth. I. 1. 160.

Sallet, *sb.* a close-fitting helmet. 2 H VI. IV. 10. 11. A salad. 2 H VI. IV. 10. 8.

Salt, *sb.* salt-cellar. Two G. III. 1. 354. *adj.* lecherous. M. for M. V. 1. 399. Stinging, bitter. T. & C. I. 3. 371.

Salutation, *sb.* give salutation to my blood = make my blood rise.

Salute, *v.t.* to meet. John, II. 1. 590. To affect. H VIII. II. 3. 103.

Sanded, *adj.* sandy-coloured.

Say, *sb.* a kind of silk.

Scald, *adj.* scurvy, scabby. H V. V. 1. 5.

Scale, *v.t.* to put in the scales, weigh.

Scall = scald. M.W.W. III. 1. 115.

Scamble, *v.i.* to scramble.

Scamel, *sb.* perhaps a misprint for seamell, or seamew.

Scantling, *sb.* a scanted or small portion.

Scape, *sb.* freak, escapade.

Sconce, *sb.* a round fort. H V. III. 6. 73. Hence a protection for the head. C. of E. II. 2. 37. Hence the skull. Ham. V. 1. 106. *v.r.* to ensconce, hide. Ham. III. 4. 4.

Scotch, *sb.* notch. *v.t.* to cut, slash.

Scrowl, *v.i.* perhaps for to scrawl.

Scroyles, *sb.* scabs, scrofulous wretches.

Scrubbed, *adj.* undersized.

Scull, *sb.* shoal of fish.

Seal, *sb.* to give seals = confirm, carry out.

Seam, *sb.* grease, lard.

Seconds, *sb.* an inferior kind of flour.

Secure, *adj.* without care, confident.

Security, *sb.* carelessness, want of caution.

Seedness, *sb.* sowing with seed.

Seel, *v.t.* to close up a hawk's eyes.

Self-admission, *sb.* self-approbation.

Semblative, *adj.* resembling, like.

Sequestration, *sb.* separation.

Serpigo, *sb.* tetter or eruption on the skin.

Sessa, *int.* exclamation urging to speed.

Shard-borne, *adj.* borne through the air on shards.

Shards, *sb.* the wing cases of beetles. A. & C. III. 2. 20. Potsherds. Ham. V. I. 254.

Sharked up, *p.p.* gathered indiscriminately.

Shealed, *p.p.* shelled.

Sheep-biter, *sb.* a malicious, niggardly fellow.

Shent, *p.p.* scolded, rebuked. M.W.W. I. 4. 36.

Shive, *sb.* slice.

Shog, *v.i.* to move, jog.

Shore, *sb.* a sewer.

Shrewd, *adj.* mischievous, bad.

Shrewdly, *adv.* badly.

Shrewdness, *sb.* mischievousness.

Shrieve, *sb.* sheriff.

Shrowd, *sb.* shelter, protection.

Siege, *sb.* seat. M. for M. IV. 2. 98. Rank. Ham. IV. 7. 75. Excrement. Tp. II. 2. III.

Significant, *sb.* sign, token.

Silly, *adj.* harmless, innocent. Two G. IV. I. 72. Plain, simple. Tw.N. II. 4. 46.

Simular, *adj.* simulated, counterfeited. Cym. V. 5. 20. *sb.* simulator, pretender. Lear, III. 2. 54.

Sitch, *adv.* and *conj.* since.

Skains-mates, *sb.* knavish companions.

Slab, *adj.* slabby, slimy.

Sleeve-hand, *sb.* wristband.

Sleided, *adj.* untwisted.

Slipper, *adj.* slippery.

Slobbery, *adj.* dirty.

Slubber, *v.t.* to slur over, do carelessly.

Smatch, *sb.* smack, taste.

Sneak-cup, *sb.* a fellow who shirks his liquor.

Sneap, *v.t.* to pinch, nip. L.L.L. I. 1. 100. *sb.* snub, reprimand. 2 H IV. II. 1. 125.

Sneck up, contemptuous expression = go and be hanged.

Snuff, *sb.* quarrel. Lear, III. 1. 26. Smouldering wick of a candle. Cym. I. 6. 87. Object of contempt. A.W. I. 2. 60. Take in snuff = take offence at. L.L.L. V. 2. 22.

Sob, *sb.* a rest given to a horse to regain its wind.

Solidare, *sb.* a small coin.

Sonties, *sb.* corruption of saints.

Sooth, *sb.* flattery.

Soothers, *sb.* flatterers.

Sophy, *sb.* the Shah of Persia.

Sore, *sb.* a buck of the fourth year.

Sorel, *sb.* a buck of the third year.

Sort, *sb.* rank. M.A. I. 1. 6. Set, company. R III. V. 3. 316. Manner. M. of V. I. 2. 105. Lot. T. & C. I. 3. 376.

Sort, *v.t.* to pick out. Two G. III. 2. 92. To rank. Ham. II. 2. 270. To arrange, dispose. R III. II. 2. 148. To adapt. 2 H VI. II. 4. 68. *v.i.* to associate. V. & A. 689. To be fitting. T. & C. I. 1. 109. Fall out, happen. M.N.D. III. 2. 352.

Souse, *v.t.* to swoop down on, as a falcon.

Sowl, *v.t.* to lug, drag by the ears.

Span-counter, *sb.* boy's game of throwing a counter so as to strike, or rest within a span of, an opponent's counter.

Speed, *sb.* fortune, success.

Speken = speak.

Sperr, *v.t.* to bar.

Spital, *sb.* hospital.

Spital house, *sb.* hospital.

Spleen, *sb.* quick movement. M.N.D. I. 1. 146. Fit of laughter. L.L.L. III. 1. 76.

Spot, *sb.* pattern in embroidery.

Sprag, *adj.* sprack, quick, lively.

Spring, *sb.* a young shoot.

Springhalt, *sb.* a lameness in horses.

Spurs, *sb.* the side roots of a tree.

Squandering, *adj.* roving, random. As II. 7. 57.

Square, *sb.* the embroidery about the bosom of a smock or shift. W.T. IV. 3. 212. Most precious square of sense = the most sensitive part. Lear, I. 1. 74.

Square, *v.i.* to quarrel.

Squash, *sb.* an unripe peascod.

Squier, *sb.* square, rule.

Squiny, *v.i.* to look asquint.

Staggers, *sb.* giddiness, bewilderment. A.W. II. 3. 164. A disease of horses. T. of S. III. 2. 53.

Stale, *sb.* laughing stock, dupe. 3 H VI. III. 3. 260. Decoy. T. of S. III. 1. 90. Stalking-horse. C. of E. II. 1. 101. Prostitute. M.A. II. 2. 24. Horse-urine. A. & C. I. 4. 62.

Stamp, *v.t.* to mark as genuine, give currency to.

Standing, *sb.* duration, continuance. W.T. I. 2. 430. Attitude. Tim. I. 1. 34.

Standing-tuck, *sb.* a rapier standing on end.

Staniel, *sb.* a hawk, the kestrel.

Stare, *v.i.* to stand on end.

State, *sb.* attitude. L.L.L. IV. 3. 183. A chair of state. I H IV. II. 4. 390. Estate, fortune. M. of V. III. 2. 258. States (pl.) = persons of high position. John, II. 1. 395.

Statute-caps, *sb.* woollen caps worn by citizens as decreed by the Act of 1571.

Staves, *sb.* shafts of lances.

Stead, *v.t.* to help.

Stead up, *v.t.* to take the place of.

Stelled, *p.p.* fixed. Lucr. 1444. Sonn. XXIV. 1. Starry. Lear, III. 7. 62.

Stickler-like, *adj.* like a stickler, whose duty it was to separate combatants.

Stigmatic, *adj.* marked by deformity.

Stillitory, *sb.* a still.

Stint, *v.i.* to stop, cease. R. & J. I. 3. 48. *v.t.* to check, stop. T. & C. IV. 5. 93.

Stock, *sb.* a dowry. Two G. III. 1. 305. A stocking. Two G.
III. 1. 306; 1 H IV. II. 4. 118. A thrust in fencing.
M.W.W. II. 3. 24. *v.t.* to put in the stocks. Lear, II. 2.
333.

Stomach, *sb.* courage. 2 H IV. I. 1. 129. Pride. T. of S. V. 2.
177.

Stomaching, *sb.* resentment.

Stone-bow, *sb.* a cross-bow for shooting stones.

Stoop, *sb.* a drinking vessel.

Stricture, *sb.* strictness.

Stride, *v.t.* to overstep.

Stover, *sb.* cattle fodder.

Stuck, *sb.* a thrust in fencing.

Subject, *sb.* subjects, collectively.

Subscribe, *v.i.* to be surety. A.W. III. 6. 84. Yield, submit. 1
H VI. II. 4. 44. *v.t.* to admit, acknowledge. M.A. V. 2. 58.

Subtle, *adj.* deceptively smooth.

Successantly, *adv.* in succession.

Sufferance, *sb.* suffering. M. for M. II. 2. 167. Patience. M.
of V. I. 3. 109. Loss. Oth. II. 1. 23. Death penalty. H V.
II. 2. 158.

Suggest, *v.t.* to tempt.

Suit, *sb.* service, attendance. M. for M. IV. 4. 19. Out of
suits with fortune = out of fortune's service.

Supervise, *sb.* inspection.

Suppliance, *sb.* pastime.

Sur-addition, *sb.* an added title.

Surmount, *v.i.* to surpass, exceed. 1 H VI. V. 3. 191. *v.t.* to
surpass. L.L.L. V. 2. 677.

Sur-reined, *p.p.* overridden.

Suspect, *sb.* suspicion.

Swarth, *adj.* black. T.A. II. 3. 71. *sb.* swath. Tw.N. II. 3. 145.

Swoopstake, *adv.* in one sweep, wholesale.

Tag, *sb.* rabble.

Take, *v.t.* to captivate. W.T. IV. 3. 119. Strike. M.W.W. IV.
4. 32. Take refuge in. C. of E. V. 1. 36. Leap over. John,

V. 2. 138. Take in = conquer. A. & C. I. 1 .23. Take out = copy. Oth. III. 3. 296. Take thought = feel grief for. J.C. II. 1. 187. Take up = get on credit. 2 H VI. IV. 7. 125. Reconcile. Tw.N. III. 4. 294. Rebuke. Two G. I. 2. 134.

Tallow-keech, *sb.* a vessel filled with tallow.

Tanling, *sb.* one tanned by the sun. John, IV. 1. 117. Incite. Ham. II. 2. 358.

Tarre, *v.t.* to set on dogs to fight.

Taste, *sb.* trial, proof. *v.t.* to try, prove.

Tawdry-lace, *sb.* a rustic necklace.

Taxation, *sb.* satire, censure. As I. 2. 82. Claim, demand. Tw.N. I. 5. 210.

Teen, *sb.* grief.

Tenable, *adj.* capable of being kept.

Tend, *v.i.* to wait, attend. Ham. I. 3. 83. Be attentive. Tp. I. 1. 6. *v.t.* to tend to, regard. 2 H VI. I. 1. 204. Wait upon. A. & C. II. 2. 212.

Tendance, *sb.* attention. Tim. I. 1. 60. Persons attending. Tim. I. 1. 74.

Tender, *v.t.* to hold dear, regard. R III. I. 1. 44. *sb.* care, regard. 1 H IV. V. 4. 49.

Tender-hefted, *adj.* set in a delicate handle or frame.

Tent, *sb.* probe. T. & C. II. 2. 16. *v.t.* to probe. Ham. II. 2. 608. Cure. Cor. I. 9. 31.

Tercel, *sb.* male goshawk.

Termless, *adj.* not to be described.

Testerned, *p.p.* presented with sixpence.

Testril, *sb.* sixpence.

Tetchy, *adj.* irritable.

Tetter, *sb.* skin erruption. Ham. I. 5. 71. *v.t.* to infect with tetter. Cor. III. 1. 99.

Than = then, Lucr. 1440.

Tharborough, *sb.* third borough, constable.

Thick, *adv.* rapidly, close.

Thirdborough, *sb.* constable.

Thisne, perhaps = in this way. M.N.D. I. 2. 48.

Thoughten, *p.p.* be you thoughten = entertain the thought.

Thrall, *sb.* thraldom, slavery. Pass. P. 266. *adj.* enslaved. V. & A. 837.

Three-man beetle, a rammer operated by three men.

Three-man songmen, three-part glee-singers.

Three-pile, *sb.* the finest kind of velvet.

Three-piled, *adj.* having a thick pile. M. for M. I. 2. 32. Superfine (met.). L.L.L. V. 2. 407.

Tickle, *adj.* unstable. 2 H VI. I. 1. 216. Tickle of the sere, used of lungs readily prompted to laughter; literally hair-triggered. Ham. II. 2. 329.

Ticklish, *adj.* wanton.

Tight, *adj.* swift, deft. A. & C. IV. 4. 15. Water-tight, sound. T. of S. II. 1. 372.

Tightly, *adv.* briskly, smartly.

Time-pleaser, *sb.* time server, one who complies with the times.

Tire, *sb.* headdress. Two G. IV. 4. 187. Furniture. Per II. 2. 21.

Tire, *v.i.* to feed greedily. 3 H VI. I. 1. 269. *v.t.* make to feed greedily. Lucr. 417.

Tisick, *sb.* phthisic, a cough.

Toaze, *v.t.* to draw out, untangle.

Tod, *sb.* Twenty-eight pounds of wool. *v.t.* to yield a tod.

Toged, *adj.* wearing a toga.

Toll, *v.i.* to pay toll. A.W. V. 3. 147. *v.t.* to take toll. John, III. 1. 154.

Touch, *sb.* trait. As V. 4. 27. Dash, spice. R III. IV. 4. 157. Touchstone. R III. IV. 2. 8. Of noble touch = of tried nobility. Cor. IV. 1. 49. Brave touch = fine test of valour. M.N.D. III. 2. 70. Slight hint. H VIII. V. 1. 13. Know no touch = have no skill. R II. I. 3. 165.

Touse, *v.t.* to pull, tear.

Toy, *sb.* trifle, idle fancy, folly.

Tract, *sb.* track, trace. Tim. I. 1. 53. Course. H VIII. I. 1. 40.

Train, *v.t.* to allure, decoy. 1 H VI. I. 3. 25. *sb.* bait, allurement. Mac. IV. 3. 118.

Tranect, *sb.* ferry, a doubtful word.

Translate, *v.t.* to transform.

Trash, *v.t.* lop off branches. Tp. I. 2. 81. Restrain a dog by a trash or strap. Oth. II. 1. 307.

Traverse, *v.i.* to march to the right or left.

Tray-trip, *sb.* a game at dice, which was won by throwing a trey.

Treachors, *sb.* traitors.

Treatise, *sb.* discourse.

Trench, *v.t.* to cut. Two G. III. 2. 7. Divert from its course by digging. H IV. III. 1. 112.

Troll-my-dames, *sb.* the French game of *trou madame*, perhaps akin to bagatelle.

Tropically, *adv.* figuratively.

True-penny, *sb.* an honest fellow. Ham. I. 5. 150.

Try, *sb.* trial, test. Tim. VI. 1. 9. Bring to try = bring a ship as close to the wind as possible.

Tub, *sb.* and tubfast, *sb.* a cure of venereal disease by sweating and fasting.

Tuck, *sb.* rapier.

Tun-dish, *sb.* funnel.

Turk, to turn Turk = to be a renegade. M.A. III. 4. 52. Turk Gregory = Pope Gregory VII. 1 H IV. V. 3. 125.

Twiggen, *adj.* made of twigs or wicker.

Twilled, *adj.* perhaps, covered with sedge or reeds.

Twire, *v.i.* to twinkle.

Umber, *sb.* a brown colour.

Umbered, *p.p.* made brown, darkened.

Umbrage, *sb.* a shadow.

Unaneled, *adj.* not having received extreme unction.

Unbarbed, *adj.* wearing no armour, bare.

Unbated, *adj.* unblunted.

Unbraced, *adj.* unbuttoned.

Uncape, *v.i.* to uncouple, throw off the hounds.

Uncase, *v.i.* to undress.

Unclew, *v.t.* to unwind, undo.

Uncolted, *p.p.* deprived of one's horse. 1 H IV. II. 2. 41.

Uncomprehensive, *adj.* incomprehensible.

Unconfirmed, *adj.* inexperienced.

Undercrest, *v.t.* to wear upon the crest.

Undertaker, *sb.* agent, person responsible to another for something.

Underwrite, *v.t.* to submit to.

Undistinguished, *adj.* not to be seen distinctly, unknowable.

Uneath, *adv.* hardly, with difficulty.

Unfolding, *adj.* unfolding star, the star at whose rising the shepherd lets the sheep out of the fold.

Unhappy, *adj.* mischievous, unlucky.

Unhatched, *p.p.* unhacked. Tw.N. III. 4. 234. Undisclosed. Oth. III. 4. 140.

Unhouseled, *adj.* without having received the sacrament.

Union, *sb.* large pearl.

Unkind, *adj.* unnatural. Lear, I. 1. 261. Childless. V. & A. 204.

Unlived, *p.p.* deprived of life.

Unpaved, *adj.* without stones.

Unpinked, *adj.* not pinked, or pierced with eyelet holes.

Unraked, *adj.* not made up for the night.

Unrecuring, *adj.* incurable.

Unrolled, *p.p.* struck off the roll.

Unseeming, *pr.p.* not seeming.

Unseminared, *p.p.* deprived of seed or virility.

Unset, *adj.* unplanted.

Unshunned, *adj.* inevitable.

Unsifted, *adj.* untried, inexperienced.

Unsquared, *adj.* unsuitable.

Unstate, *v.t.* to deprive of dignity.

Untented, *adj.* incurable.

Unthrift, *sb.* prodigal. *adj.* good for nothing.

Untraded, *adj.* unhackneyed.

Unyoke, *v.t.* to put off the yoke, take ease after labour. Ham. V. 1. 55. *v.t.* to disjoin. John, III. 1. 241.

Up-cast, *sb.* a throw at bowls; perhaps the final throw.

Upshoot, *sb.* decisive shot.

Upspring, *sb.* a bacchanalian dance.

Upstaring, *adj.* standing on end.

Urchin, *sb.* hedgehog. T.A. II. 3. 101. A goblin. M.W.W. IV. 4. 49.

Usance, *sb.* interest.

Use, *sb.* interest. M.A. II. 1. 269. Usage. M. for M. I. 1. 40. In use = in trust. M. of V. IV. 1. 383.

Use, *v.r.* to behave oneself.

Uses, *sb.* manners, usages.

Utis, *sb.* boisterous merriment.

Vade, *v.i.* to fade.

Vail, *sb.* setting (of the sun). T. & C. V. 8. 7. *v.t.* to lower, let fall. 1 H VI. V. 3. 25. *v.i.* to bow. Per. IV. Prol. 29.

Vails, *sb.* a servant's perquisites.

Vain, for vain = to no purpose.

Vantbrace, *sb.* armour for the forearm.

Vast, *adj.* waste, desolate, boundless.

Vaunt-couriers, *sb.* fore-runners.

Vaward, *sb.* vanguard. 1 H VI. I. 1. 132. The first part. M.N.D. IV. 1. 106.

Vegetives, *sb.* plants.

Velvet-guards, *sb.* velvet linings, used metaphorically of those who wear them. 1 H IV. III. 1. 256.

Veney, or venew, *sb.* a fencing bout, a hit.

Venge, *v.t.* to avenge.

Vent, *sb.* discharge. Full of vent = effervescent like wine.

Via, *interj.* away, on!

Vice, *sb.* the buffoon in old morality plays. R III. III. 1. 82. *v.t.* to screw (met.) W.T. I. 2. 415.

Vinewedst, *adj.* mouldy, musty.

Violent, *v.i.* to act violently, rage.

Virginalling, *pr.p.* playing with the fingers as upon the virginals.

Virtuous, *adj.* efficacious, powerful. Oth. III. 4 .110. Essential. M.N.D. III. 2. 367. Virtuous season = benignant influence. M. for M. II. 2. 168.

Vouch, *sb.* testimony, guarantee. 1 H VI. V. 3. 71. *v.i.* to assert, warrant.

Vizard, *sb.* mask.

Waft, *v.t.* to beckon. C. of E. II. 2. 108. To turn. W.T. I. 2. 371.

Wag, *v.i.* and *v.t.* to move, stir. R III. III. 5. 7. To go one's way. M.A. V. 1. 16.

Wage, *v.t.* to stake, risk. 1 H IV. 4. 20. *v.i.* to contend. Lear, II. 4. 210. Wage equal = be on an equality with. A. & C. v. 1. 31.

Wanion, *sb.* with a wanion = with a vengeance.

Wanton, *sb.* one brought up in luxury, an effeminate person. John, V. 1. 70. *v.i.* to dally, play. W.T. II. 1. 18.

Wappened, *p.p.* of doubtful meaning, perhaps worn out, stale.

Ward, *sb.* guardianship. A.W. I. 1. 5. Defence. L.L.L. III. 1. 131. Guard in fencing. 1 H IV. II. 4. 198. Prison, custody. 2 H VI. V. 1. 112. Lock, bolt. Tim. III. 3. 38. *v.t.* to guard. R III. V. 3. 254.

Warden-pies, *sb.* pies made with the warden, a large baking pear.

Warrantize, *sb.* security, warranty.

Warrener, *sb.* keeper of a warren, gamekeeper.

Watch, *sb.* a watch candle that marked the hours.

Watch, *v.t.* to tame by keeping from sleep.

Waters, *sb.* for all waters = ready for anything.

Wealsmen, *sb.* statesmen.

Web and pin. *sb.* cataract of the eye.

Weeding, *sb.* weeds.

Weet, *v.t.* to know.

Welkin, *sb.* the blue, the sky. Tw.N. II. 3. 61. *adj.* sky-blue. W.T. I. 2. 136.

Whiffler, *sb.* one who cleared the way for a procession, carrying the whiffle or staff of his office.

Whist, *adj.* still, hushed.

Whittle, *sb.* a clasp-knife.

Whoobub, *sb.* hubbub.

Widowhood, *sb.* rights as a widow.

Wilderness, *sb.* wildness.

Wimpled, *p.p.* blindfolded. (A wimple was a wrap or handkerchief for the neck.)

Winchester goose, *sb.* a venereal swelling in the groin, the brothels of Southwark being in the jurisdiction of the Bishop of Winchester.

Window-bars, *sb.* lattice-like embroidery worn by women across the breast.

Windring, *adj.* winding.

Wink, *sb.* a closing of the eyes, sleep. Tp. II. 1. 281. *v.i.* to close the eyes, be blind, be in the dark. C. of E. III. 2. 58.

Winter-ground, *v.t.* to protect a plant from frost by bedding it with straw.

Wipe, *sb.* a brand, mark of shame.

Wise-woman, *sb.* a witch.

Witch, *sb.* used of a man also; wizard.

Woman, *v.t.* woman me = make me show my woman's feelings.

Woman-tired, *adj.* henpecked.

Wondered, *p.p.* performing wonders.

Wood, *adj.* mad.

Woodman, *sb.* forester, hunter. M.W.W. V. 5. 27. In a bad sense, a wencher. M. for M. IV. 4. 163.

Woollen, to lie in the = either to lie in the blankets, or to be buried in flannel, as the law in Shakespeare's time prescribed.

Word, *sb.* to be at a word = to be as good as one's word.

Word, *v.t.* to represent. Cym. I. 4. 15. To deceive with words. A. & C. V. 2. 191.

World, *sb.* to go to the world = to be married. A woman of the world = a married woman. A world to see = a marvel to behold.

Wrangler, *sb.* an opponent, a tennis term.

Wreak, *sb.* revenge. T.A. IV. 3. 33. *v.t.* to revenge. T.A. IV. 3. 51.

Wreakful, *adj.* revengeful.

Wrest, *sb.* a tuning-key.

Wring, *v.i.* to writhe.

Write, *v.r.* to describe oneself, claim to be. Writ as little beard = claimed as little beard. A.W. II. 3. 62.

Writhled, *adj.* shrivelled up, wrinkled.

Wry, *v.i.* to swerve.

Yare, *adj.* and *adv.* ready, active, nimble.

Yarely, *adv.* readily, briskly.

Yearn, *v.t.* and *v.i.* to grieve.

Yellows, *sb.* jaundice in horses.

Yerk, *v.t.* to lash out at, strike quickly.

Yest, *sb.* froth, foam.

Yesty, *adj.* foamy, frothy.

Younker, *sb.* a stripling, youngster novice.

Yslaked, *p.p.* brought to rest.

Zany, *sb.* a fool, buffoon.

BIBLIOGRAPHY

Ackroyd, Peter, *Shakespeare: The Biography*, Vintage, 2006

Adamson, Jane, *Othello as Tragedy*, Cambridge University Press, 1980

Bevington, David and Bevington, Kate, *'Un Capitano Moro' in Four Tragedies*, Bantam, 1988

Bradley, A.C., *Lectures on Shakespearean Tragedy*, Penguin Classics, 2005

Halliday, F.E., *A Shakespeare Companion*, Penguin, 1964

Holden, Anthony, *William Shakespeare: An Illustrated Biography*, Little, Brown, 2002

Olivier, Laurence, *Confessions of an Actor*, Simon & Schuster, 1982

Rowse, A.L., *William Shakespeare: A Biography*, HarperCollins, 1963

Warren, Rebecca, *York Notes on Shakespeare's Othello*, Longman, 2003